The Patent

The Patent

Luke Marusiak

Rev. date: 11/15/2017

To order additional copies of this book, contact:
www.amazon.com

Also by Luke Marusiak

The Good Fight Series

Marx & Ford
Fear & Hope
Loud & Clear
Gold & Glory

Excellence in Business Leadership Series

Foundations of Excellence
Functions of Excellence
Methods of Excellence

Science Fiction

Lifeboat Moon

TO THOSE WHO REVER CREATIVE IMAGINATION.

CONTENTS

PART I BUTTON   11

PART II QUESTIONS   73

PART III SEARCH   145

PART IV CONFRONTATION   227

EPILOGUE   283

ABOUT THE AUTHOR   287

Part I

Button

1

Karma is a bitch, Jake thought as he watched the spreading blood soak into the tan carpet. His boss, Amrish Cheena, lay face down on the carpeted floor of his office. Jake stared at Amrish and felt relief. There was no way he could fire Jake now. The son of a bitch was beyond the concerns of the living. Jake's glance rose from his boss's body to the dim room.

"Is he dead?" The familiar female voice behind him asked.

"Yes."

"How can you tell?"

Jake pointed to his boss's damp crotch and touched his nose. *It has been a quarter of a century since I've seen a death rattle, but I'll never forget.* He suppressed a smile. His pompous boss was already in a decaying state. *Death robbed you of everything Amrish, including any shred of dignity.*

"Oh, that's awful . . . I smell it."

Jake faced Jiao Lui and grimaced. "When did the police say they'd be here?"

"They didn't give a time but told me not to touch anything unless he was still alive."

Jake turned back to the office. "He's not." He catalogued the scene. *There's only one person in the room,* he thought, *Amrish Cheena, and it looks like he was killed upon opening his office door.* He frowned. This unexpected turn of events was welcome, but it was also a puzzle. *The blood is still spreading, so he was just killed. But how? He looked down at the body. And why?* He crouched down, grabbed Amrish's shoulder and turned the body toward him.

"What are you doing?" Jiao asked.

"I need to see." Jake looked but wasn't sure what he saw. Amrish's neck was red and oozing blood. The top of his shirt looked blown away by an explosive. *What the hell?*

"That looks like one of his shirt buttons blew up," Jiao said behind Jake.

Jake eased his dead boss's shoulder down and stepped back from the body. *You're not very smart now, are you Amrish?* Jake lifted his gaze and examined the office. The windows were intact. He surveyed the bookshelves and the desk. There was nothing obvious amiss. *Why? Why do this?*

Jake knew, from his Desert Storm infantry division combat experience, that the emotion of loss would hit him. There was a piece of obliterated humanity lying in front of him. A person was violently and deliberately destroyed. Jake's emotional regard of the final cruelty of the killing was waiting in the wings.

Jake wanted to get answers before emotion clouded his critical thinking. He looked again at the desk and noted the absence of Amrish's laptop. That could mean nothing or it could mean everything. He heard the sound of sirens. *They're almost here.*

"Do you hear that?" Jiao asked.

"I do." Jake knew there were more details to absorb but time was running short. He turned and frowned. Jiao had returned to her workstation and was tapping away at her keyboard. *Is there nothing but cool logic with you Jiao? Don't you feel?* "Did you hear anything?"

"No. I didn't know he was in until I went to knock on his door. It swung open when I knocked and . . ."

The siren noise increased. "Do you know where his laptop is?"

"It's not on his desk?"

"No."

"Is his laptop bag beside his desk?"

Jake looked back into the office. By now the smell of defecation and reality of his boss's death was overwhelming. He looked left and right. No bag. He stepped back. "I don't see it."

The police arrived. In spite of the progressive policies of Santa Clara, California, the detective who entered the Digital Handling Systems lobby was a silver-haired middle-aged man. He went to Jiao and displayed his badge. "Where?"

Jiao lifted her hand and pointed to the office without saying a word.

"Sir, please step back."

"Okay." Jake took three steps away from the office entrance. He realized someone would have to inform Amrish's family. He absorbed that a person with hopes and fears and dreams was gone. Amrish, a person he spent the previous evening loathing and hating, was dead. Amrish, a former friend and fellow quester who turned into a betrayer and enemy, was dead.

15

The emotion hit Jake and he was thankful. His humanity was dulled, but it was still there. Tears welled in his eyes. Jake blinked and felt the warm traces on his cheeks. He glanced at Jiao as she moved beside him. She too had tear streaks. She reached out and clasped his arm. "Let's forget the pain of the past," she said. "At least for now."

He felt the sweet precision of her touch. How long had it been? Jiao's grip was firm yet soft and there was yearning in her shining eyes that melted him. "Yes," he whispered, "let's forget the pain." He hoped his tone was convincing. Jake was a long way from forgetting.

Jake went to his work station and slid into his seat. He replayed scenes in his mind of Amrish Cheena. He pushed down the recent anger and current relief. Jake remembered. Jake met the young engineer when he was just out of the U.S. Army. It was at a JMO – junior military officer – recruiting conference. Jake was bowled over by Amrish's wealth creating dreams. And Jake, like so many, caught the Silicon Valley bug.

There was worldwide fame, Marin County mansions, and untold influence for those who won in the Silicon Valley. Amrish convinced Jake, during his interview, they could share in the glory of changing the world. Jake convinced Amrish that whatever he lacked in technical background, Jake made up for in character and sheer will. It was a thirty minute interview that turned into an energizing, life changing conversation. Jake, the former U.S. Army Ranger Desert Storm veteran, patriot and career climber, believed.

Jake loved Amrish's renewable energy vision. Jake loved that his good friend from Desert Storm, Hank Rudzinski, was also in the Silicon Valley and climbing the career ladder at the semiconductor company, Processed Technologies. Hank admired his quest. That was important to Jake. Someone he looked up to admired what he was doing. Jake and Hank were the only two from the Lucky 13th, the vaunted 13th Infantry Division, that made it to the Silicon Valley. Jake and Hank were going to change the world again. Working for Amrish, Jake was going to grab the brass ring of technical achievement and everyone would know it.

Jake fell in love with Jiao Liu the moment he saw her. Jiao left Processed Technologies and joined them just four years ago. Jiao was the brilliant Caltech PhD who came to Digital Handling Systems soon after her husband passed away from cancer. Jake smiled thinking of their first months together. Jiao was like no other woman he had known. She used to run her fingers through his blonde hair and say the same of him. Jiao was a dream and a prod to greatness. He remembered the passion. Their lust was controlled up to a point and beyond that controlled point was prolonged ecstasy that seared his soul.

And then Amrish got between them. Jake wasn't sure why but all went bad and went bad fast. Jiao pulled away. Amrish, the close friend and fellow quester, became distant. When that happened, Jake floundered. He groped for ways to contribute but was dismissed at every turn.

The dismissal was the worst. Any modicum of admiration and love Jake felt turned into blinding hate. His hate had such a sharpness that when he came home from work, it took two heavy pours of single malt scotch whiskey to dull its edge. Often, Jake wouldn't stop at two.

If there was a thin line between love and hate, Jake didn't see it. The betrayal was professional and personal. It was a personal and unexplained turn. His first thoughts, on seeing Amrish lying on his office floor, were relief and joy. His betrayer had gotten his due. After the relief subsided a question posed itself and stayed persistent in front of him, why? Why was his boss killed?

His thoughts became mixed as he reminisced. He did remember the reach for the vision of a better future. He did remember the good times, the fancy lunches at Birk's and Lion & Compass, high-fiving after solving a tough problem, and mutual respect for their joint quest. Jake didn't know why it all went wrong. Emotion of mixed love and hate surged over him in a wave. He blinked and felt the tears again.

2

"I'm Detective Abbott and I'd like to take your statements," the officer said. He stood in the middle of the work area and flashed his badge a second time. He nodded at Jiao. "I'll start with you." He looked around. "Is there a conference room we can use?"

Jake felt ice in is gut. *The police are going to see me as a suspect.* He watched Jiao and Detective Abbott enter the conference room. *She'll tell them everything – our romance, the betrayal.* He wondered how much Jiao knew about their rift.

He pulled out his smartphone and scanned his emails. He didn't see any from Amrish or human resources about an exit package. *Did Jiao know Amrish was going to fire me today?* He wondered but realized it didn't matter. That he was about to be fired was simply icing on the cake. He would be a suspect no matter what.

Jake waited his turn to be questioned. He thought it best if he be helpful to the police but not too helpful. He resolved to keep the fact he was about to get fired to himself unless asked. He resolved to answer the detective's questions in as terse a manner as possible. He would add no unasked detail. *I'll answer with just a yes or no if I can.*

Jake looked at the shapes behind the frosted conference room glass. Jake and Amrish, when they were still cordial partners, had ensured the room was soundproof. Jake now wished they hadn't. He didn't even hear muffled sounds of the conversation between the detective and Jiao. Whatever she decided to say would stay in that conference room.

He stared at the shadows behind the frosted glass and frowned. The puzzle remained. Why did this happen? Why was Amrish killed? That was a critical question. If he couldn't come up with an answer, how could the police? He thought of his boss.

Amrish had been secretive of late. He would disappear for days on end and claim his absences were due to sickness or travel or some other household emergency. Jake first suspected that Amrish and Jiao were departing for mid-day trysts but that proved false. Most of the time when Amrish was absent, Jiao was still at her workstation or in the lab, toiling away.

Jake thought of the view when he turned Amrish over. Jiao said his button exploded. It appeared that way but why did Jiao say it with only a glance and with such certainty? Bleeding out because a button exploded on your neck wasn't common. Now that he thought about it, Jake never heard of such a thing. Yet Jiao knew in a moment with no more than a glance that one of Amrish's buttons exploded. Was it possible she did this? Was it possible Jiao killed Amrish?

He asked himself if the woman he shared a bed with for two years was capable of murder. *No, no way. Jiao is many things but she'd never kill. But . . . they say you can never know a person.* There were parts of Jake, dark parts, that Jiao never knew. It was a certainty there were things about Jiao that he didn't know. Was it possible? He shook his head. *No, Jiao didn't kill Amrish.* There was no way for him to believe that. But he knew he didn't do it. And if not Jake or Jiao then who? Who would want to kill Amrish?

Jiao and Detective Abbott appeared. "Thank you Doctor Liu," the detective said. "Please have everyone leave their workstations and clear the building. Our CSU – crime scene unit – has just arrived. We've already notified the Santa Clara Crime lab and they're on the way with members of our REACT – rapid enforcement allied computer team task force. We want everything preserved as is. We're treating this whole building as a crime scene."

"Okay detective," Jiao replied.

Detective Abbot turned to Jake. "I need a statement from you."

"Okay." Jake entered the conference room and shuddered as the detective closed the door. He hoped his cheeks were still damp from tears. He sat and cleared his throat. "The REACT team is for computer forensics? Are they going to search our emails?"

"Please cooperate. I need you to answer my questions."

"Okay." This wasn't a good start. After months of coldness from both Amrish and Jiao, he could use a little compassion in the midst of this tragedy. He stared across the conference room table at the detective. There'd be no kindness here.

"Tell me about your relationship with the deceased."

Jake, braced to only give a yes or no answer, paused. "I . . . um . . . I joined Amrish at Digital Handling Systems to launch products in the renewable energy space."

"How did you meet?"

"Meet? I met him at a recruiting conference when I got out of the U.S. Army."

"Veteran? Thank you for you service. What unit were you with?"

What kind of questions are these? "I served with the Lucky 13th, the 13th Infantry Division."

"What was your highest military award?"

"I got a bronze star for service in Desert Storm."

"Impressive. An infantry division combat veteran." The detective made some notes in a small pad. He looked up. "What was your relationship to the lovely lady I just met, Doctor Jiao Liu?"

"My relationship? I worked with Jiao. We worked on expanding our product portfolio from energy efficiency software to . . . you know . . . bigger stuff."

"Did you have a personal relationship with Doctor Jiao Liu outside the office?" The detective used Jiao's full PhD title with a hint of mockery.

"A personal relationship?"

"Did you have a romantic relationship with Doctor Jiao Liu?"

There it was. The direct question. "Yes."

"How long were you and Doctor Liu in this romantic relationship?"

Jake wondered what Jiao told him. "Um . . . about two years."

"When Doctor Liu started a romantic relationship with Amrish, how did you feel?"

"How did I feel? I was pretty unhappy about it." *I felt like killing the son of a bitch.* Jake prayed his flash of anger didn't show.

"Hmmm. And what do you think about how Amrish was murdered?"

"I'm not sure how he was murdered."

"You didn't look at the body?"

"I looked and saw he had cuts on his neck. I'm not sure how that happened."

"I see. Let me recap. You're an army combat veteran who watched his boss take his girlfriend away and that boss now lies dead." Detective Abbott took a sip of water. Jake realized the detective had helped himself to one of the six water bottles always stocked in the middle of the conference room table. Jake resisted the urge to take a bottle for himself. The detective took another sip and let the damning recap hang in the air. He smiled and opened his hands palms up to Jake. "You can see how you're a person of interest."

Jake stared at the detective. "Yes, I can see that."

"Was your business doing well? Were you making money?"

"No, we were losing money. We needed to hit it big with a new product."

"Did you have a new product?"

"We had several in the works."

"Were any about to be launched?"

Jake shook his head. "We were six months away from launching anything new. Even that product is only an evolution to our dated efficiency software."

The detective closed his notepad. "Can you think of a motive for someone to murder Amrish other than the interoffice love triangle you had going?"

Love triangle? The words struck Jake. "Look . . . I don't know but there has to be something else." Jake heard doors opening and muffled discussions.

"It sounds like the reinforcements are here." The detective stood. "Let's hope for your sake our investigation finds something else. Don't leave town. We'll be talking to you again."

3

Jake left the Digital Handling Systems building drenched in sweat. He went straight to the parking lot. His phone beeped the new text message tone as he slid into his red 2012 Chevrolet Camaro throwback muscle car. He looked at his smartphone and read aloud the text he'd just received. "Meet me at my place – important." It was from Jiao. That's exactly where he wanted to go. He needed to talk to Jiao. He needed answers.

Jake drove into stop-go traffic on northbound Highway 101. His heart raced and he dripped sweat in spite of his car's air conditioning blowing on the max setting. *Detective Abbott thinks I killed Amrish. And he's looking for proof.* He moved forward a car length and stopped. *He'll find on the computer systems that I was about to be fired. Then he'll have a bigger motive.* The line of traffic surged forward and Jake accelerated to keep pace.

The trip was arduous torture and as Jake perspired in the packed traffic he asked himself again. *Is it possible Jiao killed Amrish?* Jiao had the technical chops to come up with an exploding button – if that's what it really was. And no one knew Jiao that well. Her personality was distant. He thought that distance was due to her cold determination. Jake saw that coldness over and again. Hell, he admired it.

It was possible. No matter how he felt about it, no matter how he felt about Jiao, she was one person who could do this exotic killing. He could be driving into a trap. Anything was possible. What's more, if he had to ask himself about Jiao after working with her for years, what were the police going to think?

The traffic started and stopped. Jake's thoughts spread in different directions. Without the love triangle, the killing didn't make sense. Critical thinking was necessary to solve this puzzle. Jake tried to think of other possibilities. But he struggled to come up with other killers because if not Jiao, then who? And why?

Why was a good question. Why murder Amrish? Why? If he could find that out, he could figure out where to look. If Jake could figure that out, he could point the police in a different direction. Right now Jake knew, Detective Abbott was looking at him. The police were asking questions and it was inevitable they conclude the only two who could've killed Amrish this morning were Jake and Jiao. Maybe Jake or Jiao but no one else.

Jake pulled into a parking space at Jiao's townhouse. He knew Jiao had money and he knew she was careful in how she spent it. This modest Palo Alto townhouse was a good example. He bounded up the stairs to the second floor and pushed Jiao's doorbell. *I need to be on the lookout for danger.*

The door swung open and Jake gasped at Jiao's tear-streaked face. Jiao waved him in. He came in and closed the door behind him. Jiao wrapped her arms around him, buried her head in his shoulder, and sobbed. Jake held her, relished the familiar scent of her perfume, and felt ashamed for thinking she could be the killer.

Jiao pulled her head back, sobbed, and stared into Jake's eyes. "I need you," she whispered.

"I'm here."

"I'm glad." She forced a smile. "I'm sorry for how things happened."

"Me too. Do you have any idea why this happened?"

Jiao nodded. "I wanted to show you something before the police found it."

"What's that?"

Jiao went to the coffee table and got her smartphone. She tapped the screen a few times and gave it to Jake. "Look."

Jake took the smartphone. "You got a text message from Amrish at 1:34 a.m. this morning titled danger?"

"Open it."

Jake tapped the message and read. "The wrong people found out about my philosopher's stone patent. I'm in danger. Please love, secure the patent if something happens to me." He lowered the phone and suppressed a jolt at the word 'love' in the message. "What does this mean? What is the philosopher's stone patent?"

"I don't know."

"Well I sure don't know." Jake looked at the message again. "We were scouring all the renewable technology websites for ideas. I thought that's what we were looking for – an idea. This message indicates a specific patent." He looked at her. "What were you guys working on?"

"I was working on high efficiency solar panels using thin film deposition."

"I know about that. What else?"

She shook her head. "Everything else was for the software to balance solar panel efficiency loads on cloudy days."

"I know about that too. There has to be something more."

"Like you said, we were scouring all sources for ideas of a technology breakthrough. After China crashed the price of silicon solar cells, we needed new technology. We needed something we could patent and protect."

"You must have come up with something."

"We looked everywhere. We looked what DOE – the Department of Energy – was doing. We looked at what Germany was doing. We looked at what Singapore and China were doing. There's a lot of technology out there."

"You have no idea what Amrish meant by the philosopher's stone patent?"

"I don't."

"Amrish trusted you could find it."

"I need your help," Jiao pleaded. "Will you help me?"

Jake had never seen Jiao so vulnerable. And, whether he liked it or not, they were in this together. "I'll help you."

"But . . . can you trust me?"

"That's a hell of a question Jiao." He noted her pained expression. "If I help you, does it matter if I trust you?"

"Yes," she whispered. "It matters."

"I want to. Hell, I need to but it's not that easy." He exhaled. "First, tell me why."

"Why what?"

"Why did you drop me for Amrish? You never told me. I was so into you and you left me . . . for him. I'm still licking those wounds."

"Did you hate Amrish?"

"He wasn't who I thought he was. Neither of you were." He stared at Jiao. "Why did you drop me for him?"

"You don't know?"

"No, I don't know."

"You hurt me first when you blamed me for the solar cell production throughput problem."

"What are you talking about?"

"The meeting with Urban Solar – you blamed me for losing that contract."

Jake struggled to understand. "It wasn't blame. The production speed made the thin film solution uncompetitive on cost. It wasn't blame, it was fact."

"You stood up in front of a potential customer and blamed me. The problem was much bigger than throughput. I could have crawled under a rock."

Jake remembered the meeting. At the time, he was disgusted with Amrish. He was disgusted that Amrish's promise of a cost effective solution was based on a lie. It was Amrish he directed his comments toward, not Jiao. But now, he could see it. He could see how Jiao took the brunt of that criticism. He saw her eyes shine. "Jiao, I had no idea."

"Amrish did. He knew you hurt me."

"He was much more at fault than you." Jake glared. "Amrish came sailing in to comfort you after we lost Urban Solar." Jake shook his head. "Jiao we should've talked about it. You never told me this."

Jiao scowled. "I never should've had to."

Jake processed the new revelation. He faced Jiao, reached down, and clasped her hands. "I'm sorry. And I'm sorry for being too thick-skulled to know." He gazed into her eyes so there could be no misunderstanding. "I will do my level best to trust you. If you return that trust, I'll trust you with my life. That's how I'm built. This only works if we're in this together." Jiao's face lit up and Jake's heart skipped a beat. "Do you trust me?" Jake asked.

Jiao stared at him a long moment and then nodded. "I do. Thank you."

"Then let's figure out what this philosopher's stone patent is all about."

"The police don't know about this text message."

"Let them find it on their own." He looked around the pristine organized townhouse. Jiao's feng shui personality was stamped on everything inside and on each room's arrangement. Jake didn't want to leave. He turned to her. "I can sleep on the couch. Do you want me stay while we figure this out?"

"You don't need the couch. I have a spare bedroom." She smiled. "Can you stay?"

"Yes."

4

"Should we drive to the police station in separate cars?" Jake asked. He stood next to Jiao in her covered townhouse parking lot. He both wondered at and appreciated the speed he and Jiao resumed their friendship. It would take time to rebuild trust. Jake stayed in the spare bedroom but was warmed to see her morning smile.

Jiao stood arms folded staring at her car. "Why? With all the security cameras, they'll find out you spent the night."

That was true. No point hiding it. "Let's go."

Jake drove Jiao's black BMW to the police station. They were both called by the police. Jiao was called at eight o'clock. Jake was called five minutes later. The police administrator told them two things. One, the Digital Handling Systems office was still off limits and two, their presence was expected at the police station at nine o'clock.

Jake parked in the Santa Clara police station's visitor's parking space and the two got out. Jake always appreciated Jiao's dress and demeanor and now, more than ever, she displayed crisp professionalism. She was dressed in a navy blue pants suit complemented with patent leather shoes. Her waist length black hair was combed straight and her gold Rolex watch glistened. She once was the epitome of Jake's perfect woman. He wondered if she could be so again.

They entered the police station and were met at the door by Detective Abbott. "I see you two came in together. Perhaps I only needed to make one call this morning."

Jake ignored the bait. Jiao folded her arms and regarded the detective with disgust.

Another man came alongside Abbott. "This is Detective Delgado," Detective Abbott said. "The two of us will be conducting your interviews today."

"How long will this take?" Jake asked. He wanted to search for the philosopher's stone patent and they couldn't do anything while sequestered at the police station. Jake also wanted to ask a friend for help. That thought occurred to him while pondering his predicament last night. There was only one friend he could trust with something this big.

"It'll take as long as it takes," Detective Delgado answered. He shrugged. "Follow us please."

Detective Abbott escorted Jiao into one interview room and Detective Delgado escorted Jake into another. Jake was able to lock eyes for a brief moment with Jiao and noted her determination. *I'll match that attitude.*

"Can I get you a bottle of water or some coffee?" Detective Delgado asked.

"Water will be great."

The detective opened a small refrigerator in the corner of the room and extracted two water bottles. He set one in front of Jake and kept the other. "You two are really something," the detective said.

"How's that?"

"Driving in together the day after your boss was murdered."

"We needed to console one another."

"I suppose that's better than congratulating each other."

"This is a big loss for both Jiao and I. Can you share what your investigation found?"

"I can't tell you anything you don't already know."

"Do you have any idea why Amrish was killed?"

"Murdered . . . Amrish was murdered in cold blood by those with a motive. He was murdered by those who planned carefully and knew something about technology."

Jake inhaled. "Do you have an idea as to why Amrish was murdered?"

"There is the love triangle Amrish had going with Doctor Liu and you. That's a powerful motive. You two certainly have the technical expertise to do something like this."

"Something like what? How did he die?"

"You know as well as I do. Jiao confessed as much yesterday. You violated police instruction and turned Amrish over to have a look-see. You had to make sure your ingenious exploding button finished the job." He unscrewed the cap off his water bottle and took a sip. "The tears yesterday were a nice touch."

"I rolled Amrish over to make sure he was beyond help."

"Really? Am I to believe an army combat vet like you couldn't tell he was dead the moment you smelled his shit? I don't buy it. You just looked, made sure, and put him back."

Jake's anger rose. "I had nothing to do with this."

"Oh, so it was your girlfriend?"

"What? No."

"Okay then, I'll bite. Why was Amrish murdered?"

Jake stared at Detective Delgado but held his tongue. He and Jiao made a pact they'd keep the philosopher's stone patent message to themselves. At least until they had more information.

"No answer? You white collar criminals should stick to insider trading and embezzlement. Murder is out of your league."

Jake realized the detective was baiting him. He was running laps on the love triangle but was just as stuck as they were. "You've spent a day investigating and you have no idea."

"You and your girlfriend are looking better and better for this."

"The problem with that theory is we didn't do it."

"Who got into the office first, you or Doctor Jiao Liu?"

"Jiao."

"So assuming you didn't do it, how can you be sure she didn't?"

"She was just as surprised as I was and she cared for Amrish a lot more than I did."

"You and Amrish had a spat?"

"Yeah we did but I didn't kill him."

"Murder. He was murdered."

Jake paused. The conversation piqued a question in his mind. He looked at the detective. "How was the button activated? Did your guys look for an RF signal?"

"I'm asking the questions."

"I'll bet it was activated by a radio frequency signal. All's someone had to do was get the button on his shirt and drive by when they knew he was in the building. Jiao and I were set up as witnesses. Who cleans his shirts?"

"Slow down cowboy. I'm asking the questions."

"If you didn't find out who cleans his shirts, you're asking the wrong questions."

There was a knock on the door. "Hey you two," Detective Abbott popped his head inside. "Let's switch and compare notes."

"Sounds good," Detective Delgado replied. He got up and took his water bottle with him.

Detective Abbott went to the corner, extracted a water bottle from the refrigerator, and took a seat. "The other room doesn't have a refrigerator. I'm parched." He unscrewed the cap and drained half the water in one swig. "Ah, that's better. Where did you leave off with Detective Delgado?"

"Shirts. You need to find out who cleaned Amrish's shirts."

"Hmm . . . have you considered that Amrish's wife did his shirts?"

"His wife?"

"You didn't know he was married?"

"I've known Amrish for years and I never heard him talk about being married."

"His wife and kids stay in Mumbai most of the time."

"Wow, does . . ." Jake caught himself.

Detective Abbott laughed. "You're not good at masking emotion. The answer is no, Jiao says she didn't know Amrish was married until we told her yesterday."

Yesterday? Jake welded his lips together and kept his mouth shut.

"You better stay away from high stakes poker games. I can see by your expression she didn't tell you about Amrish being married." He laughed again. "Even after all that time together last night, she didn't tell you."

"That's not important."

"Not important? Hell hath no fury like a woman scorned."

"Which one was the scorned woman?"

"You tell me."

"I don't know.

"Both you and Doctor Jiao Liu are persons of interest in the homicide of Amrish Cheena. There are intersecting love triangles . . . or maybe they're lust triangles. You, Jiao, and Amrish were one. Amrish, Jiao, and his wife were the other. You can see how it'd be easy to figure you and Jiao had reason to rekindle your romance and take care of Amrish."

Jake rested his chin on his folded hands. "No, there's another reason for the murder."

"I'm listening."

"I don't know but the answer's out there."

"You be sure to call me if something comes to mind." Detective Abbott slid his card across the desk. "I have your number, now you have mine."

"Okay." Jake picked up the card and examined the shiny gold badge imprint. "I'll call when I come up with something."

"You better. We're likely to arrest you in a couple days just for sport if another motive doesn't come up."

5

The drive back to Palo Alto was a spirited affair. "You didn't tell me Amrish had a wife," Jake said as he pulled into traffic.

"I didn't believe it," Jiao said. "I don't believe it."

"You don't believe it?"

"Let me ask you. Was I ever married and do I have children?"

"Sure, I see pictures of your family on your desk. I see framed pictures of your daughter. She just started college, right?"

"Right. Did you ever see a single picture of Amrish's wife or children in all the time that you knew him?"

Jake paused. The traffic was already stop-go in mid-morning. "No, I only saw one picture on his desk."

"I saw it too. That was him and his dad when he graduated from Berkeley for his undergraduate degree. He stayed at Berkeley for grad school. When did he have time to get a wife and children in India?"

"You think the police are lying?"

"Somebody is."

"Could this have got him killed?"

Jiao shook her head. "That's not what his message said."

"Yeah, the philosopher's stone patent . . . and you have no idea what he meant."

"No, but I'm going to use my personal laptop and do a patent search when we get back."

"For what, philosopher's stone?"

"No, for Amrish Cheena. After hearing about his mysterious wife, I wonder what else we don't know. I wonder what he was working on when he was gone all the time. What else don't we know about?"

"I hope you get something from the patent search. I'm going to enlist the help of an old army friend."

"You're going to tell someone else about this? It better be someone you trust."

"He is. You may know him. He works at Processed Technologies."

"Who?"

"Hank Rudzinski."

"I do know him. I forgot you two were in the army together."

"Lucky 13th – 13th Infantry Division – ooo-rah!"

Jiao chuckled. "I think you can trust Hank."

Jake parked Jiao's BMW. She went into her townhouse to start the patent search. Jake watched her close the door and wondered what the knowledge of Amrish's wife was doing to her. *Secrets, secrets, secrets*, he thought. *It's always the need for secrets that get us in trouble.*

Jake slid into his Camaro and called his friend. He was pleased Hank Rudzinski agreed to an impromptu lunch. The two fellow 13th Infantry Division Desert Storm veterans met at the iconic Lion & Compass restaurant in Sunnyvale and were seated at a table in a quiet corner.

"Jake, I heard about Amrish and the homicide investigation." Hank got to the point. "What the hell is going on?"

"Hank, there's some weird stuff about this murder."

"They know it's murder?"

"I know it's murder."

"How?"

"Amrish was killed by an exploding shirt button."

Hank's fork full of lettuce stopped in mid-path to his mouth. "You saw this?"

"I saw his shirt blown away and he was still bleeding from the neck."

"And no one was around?"

"No. Jiao and I think it was triggered by an RF signal. Someone could've triggered it as they drove by."

"I've never heard of anything like that."

"First for me too."

"Any idea who would want to kill Amrish?"

"The police are looking at me."

"Why you?"

"Because Jiao and I were together and then Jiao started up with Amrish."

Hank pinned his friend with a hard stare. "Jake, do you remember our first meeting after Desert Storm in San Francisco?"

"It was at the Starbucks next to the Fifth and Mission parking garage. I do remember. You were going to Semicon in the Moscone Center for Processed Technologies. Jiao was probably there as well."

"Do you remember our talk of demons?"

Jake nodded. "I do. Your imagination is more developed than mine. I never named my demon like you did yours."

Hank locked eyes with his friend.

"What?"

"Tell me. Did you let your demon get the best of you and kill Amrish?"

Jake wasn't as upset about the direct question from his friend as he was from the police. Jake and Hank had shared enough horror to know about the darkness everyone carries inside. "No Hank. I didn't let my demon out of the cage."

Hank stared and Jake met his friend's gaze for a long moment. "Okay then. Why were you messing around with Digital Handling Systems anyway?"

"Messing around?"

"Yeah. Why did you throw in with a company whose only play was a big intellectual property technology breakthrough? You should've played to your strengths."

"My strengths? You mean my dumb bullheadedness?"

"Where's that coming from?"

"Even in the army, it was always you and the other tech heads."

"What are you talking about?"

"Don't you get it? I want this. I want the Silicon Valley brass ring. The only way I get it is with a play like Digital Handling Systems."

"Now I understand your attraction to Jiao. Doctor Liu is one of the smartest practical scientists in the valley. You know she invented the dielectric films for the dual damascene copper connections?"

Jake glared at Hank. "That's what I'm talking about. You and Jiao and Amrish . . . have a leg up on me."

"Jiao is smarter than both of us combined."

"I don't even know what that dual stuff is. Hell, I don't care. We were in renewable energy which is just as important."

"Everyone in the Silicon Valley drank the Kool-Aid on renewable energy. For every Tesla, there's ten Solyndras."

"But we're doing it different."

"How?"

"Efficiency, solar, storage, waste processing . . ."

"Jake where did that come from, a marketing brochure? Hundreds of failed companies were into those areas of renewable energy. Why do you think Amrish was murdered?"

"Jiao got a text from Amrish just before he died that he was in danger due to the philosopher's stone patent."

"What is the philosopher's stone patent?"

"I don't know. Does the philosopher's stone mean anything to you?" Jake knew Hank was a well-read self-proclaimed student of history. He hoped Hank's knowledge could be of use with this odd term.

Hank pursed his lips. "The philosopher's stone was a medieval concept. It was a quest more than anything. The philosopher's stone was the substance that turned base metals like mercury or lead into gold."

"I knew there was a reason I came to you. You always had your great books set with you, even in the mud."

"Yeah, I got a lot out of those books. I still do."

"Did the philosopher's stone produce any great insight?"

"The philosopher's stone was a quest of the alchemists. Hmm . . . some figure alchemy fathered chemistry. You know the vaunted process to turn a base material into gold was called the Magnum Opus." Hank laughed. "Maybe that's what we're looking for."

Jake didn't appreciate Hank's laugh. "Look, I'm liable to be in jail tomorrow if we don't find something. This isn't Dan Brown's Robert Langdon searching for the Holy Grail. This isn't some medieval quest. This is real. Amrish got killed, got murdered, for something real."

"But you have no idea what." Hank bit his lip and nodded. "I'll help you. But I need to be at arm's length. I do have my family to consider."

"Understood."

"You think the police are going to take you in?"

"I'm surprised they haven't yet."

"Do you see a need to hide at some point?"

Jake hadn't thought that far ahead. But now that it was mentioned . . . "Yes."

"Then we should get you burner phones. Something you only use once. The only time you call me after this lunch should be from one of those."

"You agree that we need to run or hide?"

"We?"

"Me and Jiao."

Hank nodded. "Yes, I think you need to hide. If someone smart and skilled enough to come up with an exploding button is on your tail, they're skilled enough to track your smartphone. If you and Jiao are the only two with a crack at figuring this out, you two are in danger."

"You're right."

"I'll start helping you right now. Let's get cash and go shopping."

"Thanks Hank. I knew I could count on you."

6

Jake and Hank drove in separate cars from the Lion & Compass restaurant. When Jake phoned Hank, he told Hank he wanted a catch-up lunch and had a favor to ask. The favor he asked of his old army buddy was a big one. It was nothing less than to aid and abet criminal suspects. He was pleased Hank didn't flinch. His one true friend showed his colors and agreed to help them.

The two went south on Highway 101 from Fair Oaks Avenue, took the Mathilda exit, and drove to the TechCU bank on El Camino Real. They both got $300 in cash from the automated teller machine and drove east on El Camino. Jake rolled the lunch conversation around in his mind. His stomach tightened at each stop light. *Hank's right about one thing. The only way Jiao and I are safe is if we figure this out. And fast.*

Jake followed Hank's red Mustang down Lawrence Expressway past the Costco and both took a left onto Arques Avenue. They pulled into the large Fry's Electronics parking lot. They no sooner entered when they saw a sign for cell phones and LTE tablets. Their combined six hundred dollars was enough for six phones and two tablets.

Hank insisted Jake hand over his cash and head for the parking lot. Jake was to wait by the cars while Hank used their combined cash at checkout. The idea made sense. If the police searched for purchases of burner phones, it was better that Jake's image not be on file at the checkout of Sunnyvale Fry's Electronics.

Jake marveled as he walked to his Camaro at the ease they had at getting advanced untraceable communications devices. *Law enforcement should never let people pay cash for stuff like this.* He sat in his car. After a ten minute wait he watched Hank come across the parking lot. Jake felt a pang of anxiety. *I hope this favor doesn't cause you harm.*

Jake lowered his window as his friend approached. "Go home and get some clothes," Hank said. "I'll meet you at Jiao's with this gear in about an hour."

"Okay."

"Does she know I'm coming?"

"I told her I was going to ask you for a favor."

Hank snorted. "Some favor."

Jake drove to his duplex and pushed down his discomfort of the roles he and Hank slipped into. Hank was the convoy leading captain and Jake was his loyal lieutenant. He shook his head. *Not this time Hank. This is my mission.*

Packing was easy. Jake traveled often and it took little time to load a weeks' worth of clothes and toiletries in his carry-on roller suitcase. The question was, if they had to hide, where would they go? He glanced at his apartment and noted it may not be as pristine as Jiao's but it would pass inspection. All was organized and neat. He'd been there five years and it was the stepping stone to his realized Silicon Valley dream. He closed the door and wondered when he would see it again.

Jake drove north up Highway 101 back toward Palo Alto and Jiao. He felt a wave of gratitude to have a friend like Hank. Jake would have got to the burner phone idea but it would have taken a while. Hank knew, with little information, he and Jiao would have to hide. He pulled his red Camaro next to Hank's red Mustang GT convertible and idly wondered which would win in a street race. *Stop it Jake. There's no competition between us.*

But there was. In the army Hank taught Jake all the tricks with the communications gear. Lieutenant Jake Hawes followed Captain Hank Rudzinski's orders at the U.S. Army's Fort Irwin National Training Center in the Mojave Desert and then in Desert Storm combat in Iraq and Kuwait.

After Desert Storm Jake saw Hank with his technical graduate degree move easily in this hi-tech Silicon Valley world. Jake often felt like a fish out of water in the valley. He struggled to understand technical details and knew, no matter how hard he applied himself, people like Jiao and Hank would always know more.

He bounded up the stairs and entered Jiao's townhouse. He set his suitcase down with a thump and closed the door. He was irritated at the scene in front of him. Hank and Jiao were huddled over a microscope.

"I didn't know you had a microscope in here." Jake tried to be nonchalant.

"Look at this," Jiao said.

Jake went over to the microscope and peered into the eyepiece. He adjusted the focus onto what looked like a tiny barbed ball. "What is it?"

"It's a piece of Amrish's button that I picked off the floor."

Jake stepped back from the microscope. "When did you pick this up?"

"Just before I called you over to see if Amrish was alive."

"But why did you pick it up?"

Jiao exhaled. "It's me. You know me. I have to get answers."

"And she got some," Hank added. He leaned up against the wall and crossed his arms. "I'm still trying to figure out what the hell you guys got into."

Jake turned to Jiao. "What did you find out from this button piece?"

"I have a few facts and can piece the rest together." Jiao walked up to Jake and grabbed one of his shirt buttons. "Look at this."

Jake looked at the button between Jiao's fingers. It looked like every other dress button he had seen. "Okay."

Jiao walked over to Hank and pointed to one of his shirt buttons. "Hank's shirt button looks the same as yours. Most men's shirt buttons are four hole type attached with white thread. Most are made with the same plastic resin."

"So Amrish never would've noticed if one was swapped."

"Men hardly know what color shirt they're wearing," Jiao replied. "The button is the perfect weapon."

"You're saying that barbed ball under the microscope is what cut Amrish's neck?"

"Yes. I saw two pieces from the fragment. The barbed ball you saw was intact. It's actually a hollow ball that expands into a star with micro-edges that would slice through anything with little force."

"Damn . . ."

"It gets worse," Hank said.

Jiao continued. "I believe they used a charged micro-capacitor to ignite the explosive. It went off like a shape charge and directed hundreds of these expanding barbed balls into Amrish's neck."

"Hundreds?"

"These are MEMs – microelectromechanical devices." Jiao shook her head. "This is advanced technology."

"Advanced?" Hank stepped into the middle of the room. "MEMs were first proposed by DARPA – Defense Advanced Research Projects Agency in 1986 for use in weapon technology. I remember hearing about it in my graduate program at Keesler Air Force Base. This is state of the art weaponry."

"Well the police should know I didn't do this," Jake said. "It's too technical for me."

"Jake," Hank said, "it takes multi-million dollar equipment in a facility that can handle toxic gases to produce a button like that."

"That's right," Jiao said. "It would take state of the art thin film equipment to deposit the explosive, submicron patterning equipment to make the capacitor, and micromachining reactors to produce a button like this."

"And someone would have to test it," Hank added. "It would've taken a few iterations to get the igniting radio frequency signal dialed in."

Jiao stepped away from the microscope. "Anyone who worked on producing this button would know it was a weapon."

"An assassination weapon."

Jake grasped the significance. "They always taught us to know your enemy. We have a high powered technically sophisticated enemy."

"But why?" Hank asked. "What were you guys working on? What was Amrish working on to attract an enemy like this?"

"I don't know," Jake replied. "Jiao, did you find anything else?"

"I went to the United States Patent Office and Trademark website and did a search for Amrish Cheena. It took me a while to get the search parameters right."

"And?"

"Amrish Cheena is a named inventor on 221 patents."

7

"How is that possible?" Jake asked. "Amrish didn't even have a PhD like you and he came up with 221 patents? What inventions do they cover?"

"I haven't had a chance to dig into the details." Jiao said. "I printed the list of patents and started to sort them when Hank came in. That's when we looked at the button fragment." She turned to Jake. "Hank told me the words philosopher's stone patent mean nothing."

"I didn't say that. I said it was a medieval term for the substance to turn base metals into gold. And the philosopher's stone process was called the Magnum Opus."

"Like she said," Jake replied. "The text about the philosopher's stone means nothing."

"But it can't mean nothing," Jiao said. "Amrish was killed for a reason."

"Yeah and he had an enemy with a lot of technology, resources, and reach." Hank added.

"We have an enemy with a lot of technology, resources, and reach." Jake said. "We're the ones in trouble now. We're in danger from this unknown powerful enemy and we're in danger from the police." He looked from one to the other. "The police aren't looking for our enemy. They are looking at us."

Hank stood. "This is the definition of being between a rock and a hard place." The witty observation was greeted with silence.

Jake looked to Jiao. Jake always relied on his character in adversity. He relied on his character and trusted the smartest people to get answers. Amrish's murder was different. Two of the smartest people he knew were stumped. They had no answers. Their speculation matched his own.

Maybe his character was the only thing left. *It's not the circumstance that means anything,* Jake thought. *It's never the circumstance but always the character of the man. The circumstance reveals character but it's only character that counts. What counts is how I respond, how I handle this adversity.* Jake turned to Hank. "Where did you put our burner phones?"

"He gave them to me and they're in the bedroom," Jiao replied. "Do you think hiding is a good idea?"

"The police think it was a love triangle that got Amrish killed." Jake took his suitcase to the spare bedroom and returned with the bag of burner phones.

"Jake, spending the night here after Amrish was killed wasn't the best move. If they wondered about a love triangle before, that cemented it for them."

"I spent the night because Jiao had lost her friend. We both lost a friend." He pointed to a doorway. "I stayed in the spare bedroom."

"We tried to figure out our mixed up feelings for Amrish," Jiao said. "We were trying to figure out what to do." She gazed at Jake and smiled with gratitude. "We didn't sleep much. We stayed up talking about why this happened."

"Did you come up with any answers?" Hank asked.

"We told you everything," Jake replied. "We've got to find out what Amrish meant by the philosopher's stone patent."

Hank frowned. "The police are your most urgent concern. They need to be helping you."

"They're not."

"Jiao showed me the text Amrish sent about being in danger because of that philosopher's stone patent. Did you show that message to the police?"

"No, we thought they'd find out anyway," Jiao said. "We wanted to figure out which patent Amrish's text referred to first."

"But instead of one, you found Amrish was the named inventor on 221 patents." Hank shook his head.

"How long will it take to go through 221 patents?" Jake asked.

"A while," Jiao replied. "And everything I look at will be of interest to the police if they take my computer."

"When they take your computer."

"Let's cover what we do know on the how, who, and why," Jake said. His whipsawed emotion made critical thinking difficult. "We know how Amrish was killed. Amrish was killed by a futuristic exploding button. We know the who is a powerful enemy with deep pockets and access to multi-million dollar state of the art technology. But the why is still missing. The only clue we have on the why is the text Amrish sent yesterday."

"That and Jiao's search of the patent website," Hank said.

"Are the 221 patents and that text the only thing left to go on?"

"That's all we've got."

"Let's start going through the patents."

"I've annotated the printout," Jiao said. "All appear to be related to what we were working on – renewable energy." She crossed the room and picked up a stack of papers. "Although there are a couple patents here that refer to desalination of seawater."

"Well, that makes sense," Jake said. "California is in dire need of both renewable energy and fresh water."

"Most of these patents are on renewable energy."

"What's most mean?"

"Only four are on desalination technology. The rest are where we need to focus."

Jake exhaled. "Where do you want to start?"

"Let's start looking at patents in line with products we worked on at Digital Handling Systems."

"That makes sense." Jake came alongside Jiao and regarded the printout.

Jiao's phone rang. She picked up her smartphone, looked at the caller identification, and inhaled. "It's Detective Abbott."

"You better answer," Jake said.

Jiao tapped the answer button and lifted the smartphone to her ear. "Yes, this is Doctor Liu." There was a pause and she nodded. "Yes, Jake is with me."

Jake groaned. "They're probably on the way here to arrest us."

"Yes, I understand." Jiao looked worried. "I understand." She lowered her phone, tapped the hang up button, and turned to Jake. "Detective Abbott wants us to come to the police station so they can cover what they know." She looked from Jake to Hank and back to Jake. "Should we go?"

"Yes," Jake said. "We've got to see if we can get them on our side. Having both the police and a powerful enemy against us is too much. You should show them Amrish's text about being in danger."

"Should we tell them about the button?"

"They would have figured that out already," Jake replied. He nodded. "I wonder if they'll tell us about what they found on the button."

"That's important. The button shows the sophistication of the enemy we're up against."

"You ought to print another copy of Amrish's 221 patents for the detective," Hank said. "The police wouldn't do a patent search so that's new information. That would give them a different avenue to pursue."

Jiao looked at Jake who nodded. "Okay," she said with ice in her voice, "but I need to be the one to find the philosopher's stone patent. I need to find the answer before the police."

"Why's that so important?"

"Because Amrish trusted me to find it. I owe him that."

"We can't find answers if we're in jail," Jake said.

"I'll make another printout for Detective Abbott."

Hank walked to the door. "I'm going into the office for a couple of hours. I'll meet you here later tonight."

"Hank, can you put the burner phones and tablets in your trunk?" Jake asked. "Just in case they follow us home with search warrants."

"Okay."

Jake went into the bedroom and returned with the Fry's Electronics bag. He handed it to Hank. "I hope we don't get you any deeper into this."

"Against an enemy with this kind of reach? I'm already in the thick of it." Hank looked at both. "This is what's called 'having your back'. You two are among the best people I know. I'll help you face this thing, whatever it is."

8

Jake drove Jiao in his Camaro to the police station. It was late afternoon. They had just been at the police at 9:00 a.m. and Jake was wary about coming back the same day. He noticed as he pulled into the police parking lot that Jiao, who was silent on the ride, was upset. She had streaks of tears on her cheeks, kept her chin up, and her head facing the windshield. "Hey Jiao . . ." Jake struggled to find words. "It's going to be okay."

"I can't stop thinking about what happened to Amrish. He would have been conscious for a minute or more." She wiped her eyes. "He died alone."

A wave of regret swept over Jake. He was startled to see Jiao in such pain. "You never know about these things. He may have known you found him. He knows that you're grieving for him."

"Do you really believe that?"

He stared out the windshield. "Yeah, I do. He knows."

Jake's thought gears were locked in place, bound between the woman he wanted to love and the boss he wanted to hate. He struggled to find compassion for the boss who was about to fire him. He couldn't. And, in truth, compassion didn't matter. It was the puzzle that was important. It was the why that had to be found. He turned to Jiao. "I had no idea Amrish was doing something dangerous."

"He wasn't."

"He was and he knew it. That's why he sent you the text."

Jiao lifted the printout of the 221 patents. "We need to find out why he was killed. The answer is in here somewhere."

"Let's hope the police help us."

They both jumped when Detective Delgado knocked on the driver's side window. "Hey you two," the detective said. "We're waiting."

Jake saw the detective examine their faces as they exited the car. He hoped Detective Delgado saw Jiao's tears. Delgado escorted Jake and Jiao into two separate interview rooms.

Jake noted he was in the same interview room as before – the one with a small refrigerator in the corner. Jake resisted the urge to get a bottle of water. He sat at a center table and stared at a mirror on the wall. *I wonder who's on the other side.* The room was dank and dim. His thoughts ran laps around recent events – Amrish, Jiao, Amrish's wife, Hank, philosopher's stone patent, barbed balls, named inventor on 221 patents . . . most of them about renewable energy. None of it made sense.

There was something else that stuck like a thorn in his brain. Their enemy used multi-million dollar tools to create a remotely triggered exploding button. Their enemy triggered the button in the workplace. The place of the murder was to serve a purpose. An enemy that powerful could've killed Amrish quietly when he was at home. The remote trigger would have worked just as well there as at work.

They chose to kill Amrish at work. They wanted his murder to be public. They wanted Jake and Jiao to see Amrish bleed and they wanted them to be suspects. Getting help from the police looked like a better idea the more he thought about it.

Detective Delgado came into Jake's room. "So you and Doctor Liu are a couple now."

"Not really."

"You spent the night with her, right?"

"In her townhouse but not with her. She was upset. I'm upset." Jake hated reacting to the detective's callous comments. He tried to steer the conversation. "What did you guys find out?"

"We found out you two hid a critical text message."

"We get hundreds of texts. We didn't know it was critical." Jake regretted the words the moment they left his mouth. "Look, that's not true. We wanted to see if we could figure it out."

"What did you find?"

Delgado's questions kept Jake on the defensive. "We started looking at Amrish's patents. Jiao printed a list for you."

"Yes, I know."

"There's something else. Are you sure Amrish was married?"

"You think we'd make that up?"

"He never had a picture of his wife or children on his desk. Does that make sense?"

The detective shrugged. "Different cultures . . ."

Jake cleared his throat. "Didn't you say over the phone that you'd update us on what was found? Can we go back into the Digital Handling Solutions office?"

"No, I wanted to give you a chance to come clean."

"I am coming clean."

"What do you know about how Amrish was murdered?"

"I saw blood ooze from his neck. A piece of his shirt was gone . . . like a button exploded."

"Yeah, just like that. Something pretty hi-tech, wouldn't you say?"

"I've never heard of it before."

"Yeah, we checked your background and I believe that."

A wave of anger crossed Jake's face before he could suppress it. He inhaled and exhaled a long breath. "Jiao brought a printout of 221 patents that have Amrish named as inventor. Did you get a chance to look at them?"

"Don't worry about what we're looking at. Don't you know you're being played?"

"No."

"Let's try this again. Your boss steals your girl and doesn't tell either of you he's married. Big surprise. He tells you that you're about to get fired." Detective Delgado slammed his open palm on the interview table. "That's a little detail you forgot to tell us. And Doctor Liu, something of a technical genius who has access to Amrish's clothes and smartphone on a daily basis, decides enough is enough."

"What?"

"She uses her PhD material science skills to make a killing button, uses her access to sew it on Amrish's shirt, and uses Amrish's smartphone to text herself a cryptic message. She murders her boss and lover. And, moments after doing the deed, she enlists the help of the poor sap who used to love her – you."

"That's not . . ."

"Oh but it is. We know these 221 patents are nothing but a diversion. No one in the Silicon Valley thinks Amrish was capable of coming up with a world-beating patent. Doctor Jiao Liu had means, motive, and opportunity. Everything makes sense except you. The only thing we can't figure out is if you're really as stupid as you appear."

Jake shook with rage. His reach for character, as so often happened in Silicon Valley meetings, was derailed by pompous condescension. Detective Delgado's disdain stung. "Are you arresting me?"

"Not yet. We're putting both you and Doctor Liu on passport and credit card control. If you buy so much as a paper clip, we'll know about it. We're accumulating our evidence. The only thing we still have to figure out is if you were in on it beforehand."

"There was no it to be in on." Jake was numb. He felt physically bludgeoned. "The button . . . it was made by someone powerful . . ."

"You mean someone very smart like Doctor Jiao Liu."

"No, it takes a secret facility to make a button like that."

Detective Delgado shrugged. "The Silicon Valley is full of secret facilities making exotic stuff no one's ever seen. And Doctor Liu is one of the best."

Jake remembered looking through the microscope at the barbed ball in Jiao's townhouse. He shook his head. "You've got it wrong. There's someone else, very powerful, doing this. One of those patents is the reason why."

"I have to ask you something."

"What?"

"Does it really make sense to go to bed with this woman? You're making it awful easy for her to kill you after you've served your purpose."

"Is this all?" Jake's brain was muddled. "Is this all?"

"Unless you have something more to say."

"I don't."

"Drive careful."

9

Jake drove north on Highway 101 in stop-go traffic and tried not to look at Jiao. He felt her eyes on him. Jake's shirt was again soaked with perspiration, the result of Detective Delgado's questioning. The car air conditioning didn't put a dent in the heat generated from his racing thoughts.

"What happened?" Jiao asked.

"Let me think," Jake replied. It was a cliché that the police would try to get a wedge between them. It was in all the police television shows – get the suspects to turn on each other.

"They tried to rattle you."

"They succeeded." He swallowed. "They found out Amrish was going to fire me."

Jiao started. "I didn't know that."

Jake felt drops of sweat fall from his chin and splatter on the buttons of his shirt. The buttons! The buttons that look just like the one that killed Amrish. He wrestled to analyze why he was so upset. *Focus. Focus on what triggered this flop sweat.*

"Jake, tell me what Detective Delgado said."

"He told me they're watching us and that the evidence points to you. They think the patents are a diversion. The police are not our ally. They're not even looking at the patents."

"I'm not surprised."

"They think I'm an idiot to trust you."

Jiao was silent a long moment. "What do you think?"

"I think we better find something fast."

"What do you think of me?"

"I trust you." Jake was grateful he answered without pause. He hoped Jiao believed him. "I don't know why I'm so rattled." He came to an abrupt stop due to traffic. "What did Detective Abbott tell you?"

"He said it doesn't look good for me. He asked if you put me up to this . . . you know, for revenge."

"Did he even look at the patent list?"

"Detective Abbott took the printout but he didn't think much of it."

The traffic surged forward and Jake accelerated. "Maybe that's why I'm so rattled. They have nothing to go on other than you're a technical genius and I'm the ex-boyfriend who spent the night with you after Amrish was killed."

"They don't care about the patent list. They're trying to get us to turn on each other."

"I know but Jiao, I'll never turn on you." Jake was again grateful he replied without hesitation. He did have a sliver of doubt about Jiao but if they were to have any chance at all, if he were to have any chance at all, they had to stick together.

"Maybe they just didn't tell us about the patents. Maybe they wanted to see what we know."

"Think about it Jiao. Their love-triangle story makes a lot of sense. If you heard about this happening to someone else, what would you think?"

Jiao inhaled. "We're going to be arrested."

"Unless we find something else and fast."

Jake pulled his Camaro next to Jiao's BMW in the townhouse parking lot. The two went upstairs side by side in slow strides and went inside. Jiao lowered herself in the padded seat at her desk and swiveled the chair toward Jake. "Everything I love, I lose."

Jake pulled a chair from the dining table and set it across from Jiao. He took a seat and faced her. "Hey, remember – I'm here."

"First it was Hong Kong. My family had to sell everything before the Chinese takeover in 1997."

"I remember you telling that story."

"Four generations of my family lived in Hong Kong. They built up so much. They built a future and legacy for us to carry onward. But we couldn't. We had to leave it all behind."

Jake reached across Jiao's knees and clasped both her hands.

"And then my husband, Keng, who went by Tony here, gets lung cancer. He smoked." She shrugged. "But everybody smoked. He died a year after they found the cancer." She lifted her head and met his gaze. "And I thought you loved me."

"I did Jiao. I do." Jake wondered if that were true.

"You betrayed me for the littlest thing. I can't tell you how much that hurt."

"God Jiao, I didn't know . . ."

"If you loved me, you would support me through everything. You blamed me for a production machine's low throughput in front of everybody. You didn't even talk to me."

"Jiao . . ."

"And then Amrish and I got so close. We were going use technology to change the world. All of a sudden, he pushes me away and gets murdered." She groaned. "Then I find out all that time we were together, he was married." She pulled her hands from Jake and buried her head in them. Sobs shook her.

Jake put a hand on each shoulder and pulled her toward him so her head rested on his shoulder. He had an epiphany that, in the midst of all his questions, he should trust this woman. He should love this woman. They needed each other and, even if it were nothing but need that welded them together, that was enough.

He took the leap. "Jiao, I love you and I'm sorry for the past. I'll never betray you. I'm with you in this thick and thin, no matter what happens."

Jiao sighed and shook. "What does thick and thin mean?"

"It means you can trust me, you can count on me to have your back and defend you always."

She pulled back and stared at him with tear stained eyes. Jiao searched his face. She leaned forward and the two shared a light kiss. She rested her head on his shoulder. "Okay Jake. Give me some time. Too much has happened too fast."

"I'll give you time but remember, the police won't."

Jiao sat back. "You're right. No one's going to figure this out but us." Jiao swiveled to her desk, wiped her eyes, and regarded the print out of 221 patents. "I need to sort this list."

Jake looked at the stack of papers with a measure of dread. It always came down to diving in technology he little understood. That didn't matter. Character had its dictates. "Give me half and I'll help."

Jake and Jiao sorted the patents by title. There was only one computer in Jiao's townhouse so while she worked on her laptop, Jake used his smartphone to get patent detail. After a few minutes of annotation, Jake stopped. "This looks like a fantasy list."

Jiao chuckled. "I know. I'm looking at old electrolysis technology that's labeled cold fusion."

"Cold fusion? That's was debunked in the 1980s." He flipped a page. "Look at this. Here's a patent for a static electricity generator. It's right out of Ayn Rand's book, *Atlas Shrugged*."

"None of this is viable. I'm seeing flow batteries that use old technology but have a unique apparatus, a solid oxide fuel cell, thin film solar cells using CIGS – copper indium gallium selenide deposition . . ."

"We tried that, remember?"

"So did Solyndra. Remember what happened to them?"

"The same that happened to most Silicon Valley solar companies. They died when China crashed the price of silicon." She nodded. "Chinese companies used amorphous silicon and we were using semiconductor grade silicon. We were so stupid."

Jake was jolted by the word stupid. The chip on his shoulder of being a technical dolt got heavier. He kept on task. "Look at this. Here's a patent for implant technology used to form the P-N junction of a solar cell." He felt that was an intelligent observation. "We know that's never going to be cost effective."

Jiao shook her head. "So what do we have?"

"Cold fusion, a static electricity generator, flow batteries, fuel cells, CIGS and implant solar cells."

"These renewable energy patents are repurposed old and failed technology. Even the couple patents to make fresh water are just tweaks on old desalination technology." Jiao's voice was tinged with anxiety. "You're right."

"About what?"

"None of this is worth killing for. We're in trouble."

"What do we do?"

"We have to do what the Apple billboard said: think different."

10

Arjun Azmi walked across the thick opulent carpet. He stood to the side of his large $250,000 cherry wood desk that was reputed to have belonged to robber baron Leyland Stanford. He smiled. He had all the yearned-for trappings of success. He had all the trappings of success his wife wanted.

It was time to secure their legacy. This was the moment to secure their future. They were close to finish line. Once across it the Azmi family would rival the Stanford's in wealth and influence for generations to come. *Family, future, fortune,* Arjun thought. *Our motto will be made real.*

But there was the irksome problem of Amrish Cheena. Or, to be more precise, of Amrish's employees Jiao Liu and Jake Hawes. They were digging in a list of patents and it was only a matter of time before they found the technology that could pull the rug out from Arjun's well laid plans. They had to be stopped.

Arjun relished his position and power but he wanted more. For himself, his wife, and his family . . . there was no obstacle he wouldn't bulldoze over in his quest for power. History was his guide. *The biggest mistake the British made in India,* he thought, *was they didn't kill Gandhi the moment he raised his head.*

That was the lesson of history most failed to grasp. Supremacy was about nipping problems in the bud. It was about defeating your enemies before they grew strong enough to oppose you. Ruthlessness was needed. No, even more than that, an enjoyment of that ruthlessness was required. Enemies weren't to be wounded or weakened, enemies were to be destroyed.

The senseless compassion to pardon Brutus was what got Julius Caesar killed. Arjun shook his head. Compassion was for the weak. Among all the glitter and wealth of Silicon Valley, Arjun never forgot the lessons of history. He never forgot that the glitter didn't mask the fact this was a war.

It was a win all or lose everything war for control of the future. The gap between the winners and losers would be vast. The gap would be near immeasurable. With stakes this high there was only one imperative. For family, future, and fortune, Arjun intended to win this war.

"It is time for action, not thought." Arjun's wife, Lalita, breezed in the room as if she were in a beauty pageant. In fact, a beauty pageant was where Arjun first saw her.

Arjun thought Lalita would be the testament to his achievement. That was far more important than the silly notion of love. What he soon discovered was that Lalita was a kindred spirit. She used Arjun for the very same purpose he used her. Arjun turned and regarded his wife. For all the enjoyment he got from ruthlessly destroying his enemies, it paled when compared to Lalita. "We have to stop them."

"Yes we do," Lalita answered. "These people have strange loyalties. Amrish was to isolate himself from Jake and Jiao."

"Amrish – his father was a Dalit, a worthless Untouchable – who would've thought that Amrish would find the one thing that threatens all we've built."

"Who would've thought killing Amrish wasn't enough to close the door on that threat?" Lalita had the look of a feral panther about to pounce.

Arjun leaned back in his luxurious leather padded desk chair as the captain of industry he aspired to be. "I know from my police contact that Amrish sent a text about a patent. That's what put Jiao and Jake on the trail."

"Does your contact know if they discovered the patent?"

"Not yet. From what they told the police, they've just started looking."

"But Jiao and Jake will find it, if not for loyalty to Amrish then for self-preservation."

"Yes, the pressure from the police didn't put a wedge between them as we expected. It drove them together."

"Jake and Jiao are welded into a team but that's not all. Jake enlisted a friend he knew from the army." Lalita shook her head. "This won't do."

"I am fortunate to know that much. I wish those cameras from the movie *The Circle* were in place everywhere. Then we would know everything they know. We would know everything they're doing."

"That will come. In the meantime, we must squash them like the bugs they are. What do we know about these two?"

"We know Jake and Jiao are scared. That's why they asked for help. And they're smart. They're smart enough to disappear. We may lose visibility into what they're doing."

Lalita scowled. "This won't do. Tell me again Arjun, what does our wealth and influence rest on? What is the base of our family, future, and fortune?"

"It all rests on the one thing that moves the world – power, electrical power. There's nothing more essential to civilization. There's nothing more certain to grow than the need for electrical power. In all future predictions, the world will need more electricity." Arjun opened his cigar box and inhaled the aroma. He smiled and closed the box. "Now the governments of the world, because of climate, are mandating how electric power gets generated. All we had to do to secure our position is intercept that how. Once we get the California government on our side, our future is secure."

"Your government contracts for solar farms, wind turbines, and electric car charging stations will be worthless if we don't stop this."

Arjun rose from his chair. He crossed the room and faced a low bookcase. "That's what we're trying to do." He opened a wooden lacquered box that was centered on the bookcase. Arjun regarded the nondescript men's shirt buttons and frowned. "Lalita darling, there are two buttons left. We started with six and one was used for Amrish. Where are the other three?"

Lalita glided across the room. She lifted Arjun's hand and closed the box. "It's best you leave that to me."

"I'll leave that to you and your darling little brother Laksh." Arjun glared at his wife. "You thought Amrish would be enough. Tell Laksh to be careful this doesn't get out of control."

"My brother has shown time and again that when the situation calls for lethal force, there's no one better."

"We should've nipped this in the bud by now."

"We didn't anticipate these strange loyalties."

"Our risk has grown. What about the police? They have the list of Amrish's patents."

"The police will never figure it out. You told me yourself they're discounting the patents as a diversion. The ones to stop are Jiao and Jake." She turned from the bookcase, her feral stare burned. "It'll take more than putting them in jail."

"Did you use two of the buttons on them?"

"Jiao has a daughter. Jake has an ex-wife. His friend Hank has a wife and son. We must consider their pressure points."

"Which pressure points do you plan to use?"

"I'm thinking which is best. Leave it to me . . . and Laksh." She turned back to the bookcase and drummed her fingers on the lacquered top of the wooden box containing the buttons. "I'm going to focus on the ex-soldier Jake Hawes. I'm sure he has an overdeveloped sense of honor."

"You always know how to make someone's proud strength into a debilitating weakness."

"Honor without attachment is a grave weakness. Between his misguided honor and his strange loyalties, I'll exploit Jake. I'll make him taste fear. I'll give him an idea of the power he's opposing. His honor will crumble."

"You're going to warn Jake he may get a button?"

"I'm going to threaten to take away the two closest to him, Jiao and Hank. I'm going to tell him to force a stop to the patent search or face responsibility for his friends' deaths. And before tomorrow noon, Jake will taste fear in its most primal state."

"What if the police pick them up before tomorrow noon?"

"I doubt Jake's that stupid but we can deal with that too. Fear is our ally."

Arjun stared at the impossibly beautiful woman and shuddered.

Part II

Questions

11

Jake stared at the text in disbelief. *Who? Who sent this?* His face reddened and he panted in shallow breaths. This was a bolt out of the blue – the unseen enemy just poked him in the eye.

"Jake?" Jiao asked. "What happened?"

He tried to catch his breath. He turned to Jiao. "I got a text from an unknown number."

"What does it say?"

"It says, 'Jake – stop looking for answer to Amrish's death or Jiao and Hank will die. We will save you from jail and provide proof of our reach.'" He swallowed. "They called me by name."

"They know of Hank and me?"

Jake looked at Jiao with wide eyes. "What kind of enemy has a reach like this?"

"How could they know what we're doing?"

"We only told the police we're looking at patents."

"There's a mole in the police department?"

"Has to be. There's no other way they could know we're looking at patents."

"We just told the police about the patents a few hours ago. In less than a day you get a message to stop?"

Jake calmed and engaged his brain. "This confirms it. We're looking in the right place. Amrish was killed for something in these patent filings."

The two started at a knock on the door. They heard Hank Rudzinski's voice. "It's me."

Jiao crossed the room and opened the door. Hank entered and walked up to Jake. "I just came here from my house in Needlegrass and passed by your place in South San Jose. It's swarming with police cars. You're out of time."

"Oh." Jiao exhaled.

"Did you find anything in the patent filings?" Hank asked.

"Cold fusion, fuel cells, CIGS, implant solar, a static electricity generator, flow batteries, distillation desalination . . ."

"What?"

"We don't know why Amrish was killed."

"But I got this." Jake handed Hank his smartphone.

Hank's brow furrowed as he read. "They're threatening me too? They think they can keep you out of jail? What the hell?" He pulled on the collar of his pullover shirt. "I'm not going to wear a shirt with buttons again but damn . . . only you and Jiao were in the police station. How did they find out about me?"

"The police would know about you Hank," Jiao said. "They found Amrish's philosopher's stone patent text without me telling them. They're tracking our phone calls."

"And from what we know, any information the police gets goes straight to the killer."

"We have a sophisticated powerful enemy."

Jiao took Jake's phone and stared at the threatening text. "This enemy talks of proof of their reach."

"Maybe that's why the police cars were swarming Jake's house," Hank said.

"Or maybe this townhouse is about to go up in smoke." Jake retrieved his phone. "I'm not sure what they're asking. They want us to stop searching? What does that mean? Do they want us to give ourselves up to the police?"

"It's like you said earlier Jake. We're on the right track." Jiao tapped the stacks of papers. "We are doing something that scares them."

"Well that's not good because they're the ones that scare me. We have no idea who they are. We don't have a clue as to which patent they're worried about. What the hell do we do?"

"The police will be here." Hank looked at the door. "They may be on the way right now."

"Then we should tell them everything. I'll show them the text and put it into their hands."

"Jake, remember our police interviews today." Jiao stood and faced him. "They don't believe us."

"I can't put you two in more trouble. You guys are my life."

"That's why they threatened you with Jiao and me." Hank paced. "This thing doesn't make sense. Patent filings are public information. Everyone in the Silicon Valley have been churning renewable energy patents for a decade. You gave the police a stack of patent filings and are threatened a few hours later? How is that possible?"

"Someone in the police department picked up the phone the moment we left."

"Who are these guys?" Hank looked from Jake to Jiao. "You have to have some idea. Who were you and Amrish dealing with that has this reach?"

"I don't know," Jiao said. "We've been knocking on every door in the valley for funding – Sand Hill Road, angel investors, you name it. There are dozens we've asked for funding."

"It could be any of them," Jake said. "But we never got the funding. At least I never saw it."

"I'm still stuck on why," Hank said. "How could public information garnered from a search of patent filings be dangerous? Every company worth their salt does these searches."

"You're right," Jake said. "Anyone can do what we're doing."

"And everyone does," Jiao said. "Everyone does patent searches. That's where I get a lot of my ideas." She looked at her marked up patent list.

"What's worth killing for?" Hank asked. "What has someone this paranoid? I mean, what were you guys doing over there at DHS?"

"I was working on what a lot renewable energy companies in the Silicon Valley are," Jiao answered. "Thin film high efficiency solar cells."

"And software," Jake said. "We made our money on efficiency software for metered power. But the subsidies are running out and we're losing money. DHS is on its last legs." He scowled. "Amrish got into something and pushed me away months ago. We don't know what he found."

"It takes a while to file patents," Jiao said. "Whatever he found, he found a while ago. It must have taken him months to figure out its significance. And then he pushed me away."

"We don't have months. We have hours to figure this out," Jake said. "And that's if we don't get caught."

"No one has been to DHS the last two days." Hank continued pacing. "But what you're doing now is scaring these big time powerful enemies. They thought killing Amrish would stop everything but they didn't figure he'd send Jiao a text about a philosopher's stone patent."

"That text is why I did the patent search with Amrish Cheena as named inventor."

"You told the police about 221 patent filings and the same people that killed Amrish found out. That scared them." Hank whistled. "You're scaring enemies that have the resources to produce an RF triggered exploding button." He looked from Jiao to Jake. "All you're doing is looking at the patents, right?"

"Yes, but again, only the police know that." Jake said.

"How would anyone know if we stop looking?" Jiao asked.

Jake stood. "Too many questions. We're out of time. We are threatened and police are on the way. What's our next move?"

"We need to quit gabbing and get you guys out of this townhouse." Hank said.

"Hide?"

"Jake and I should go to a hotel," Jiao said. "We'll turn off our smartphones and I'll bring my laptop."

"What will that buy us?"

"It'll buy us a day," Jiao answered. "We need time to think. Hank's right. If they're at your apartment, they'll be here soon. We should leave now."

"Okay, we leave now with both cars." He turned to his friend. "Hank are you with us?"

"Yes, where are we going?"

"Do you have any ideas of a local hotel?"

Hank pondered. "How about the Residence Inn in Sunnyvale. It's off Lakeway Drive. My family and I were put up there when we first moved to California."

"I know it. All the comforts of home."

"Will the police break down this door if we aren't here?"

"Yes, they will. We need to go."

12

Detective Delgado walked across Jake's duplex in response to his partner's call. "Did you find something?"

Detective Abbott pointed. "Look at that."

A uniformed technical crime scene investigator stepped back from the closet and, with a gloved hand, placed an electronic box on a nightstand. The box was the size of thick textbook. The investigator opened the front revealing four knobs and a dark LCD screen. "Bingo."

"What do you mean bingo?"

"What do you want to bet there's an electrical oscillator in this box and that these knobs control a generated RF signal?"

"So what?"

The investigator placed a shirt button beside the box. "I've examined this button we've found on Jake's nightstand with 1000X magnification. This little button is the murder weapon. It's chock full of little razor balls. What do you want to bet I could get it to pop with this RF generator?"

"That's how the DHS CEO, Amrish Cheena, was murdered?" There was surprise in Detective Abbott's voice. It wasn't so much that the exploding button theory was confirmed as much as the speed they confirmed it.

"That's how."

"You found an explosive button on his nightstand and the RF trigger box in his closet." Abbott frowned. "I would've figured we'd find this set up in Doctor Liu's townhouse." Detective Abbott peered at the button and the box. "Jake doesn't have the technical expertise to make a weapon like this. Why would it be here?"

"Maybe his girlfriend asked him to hide it. We know from security cameras he came here yesterday before going to Palo Alto."

"Jake knew we'd come here. He had to." Detective Abbott shook his head. "For a smart pair doing hi-tech murder, leaving the button and RF generator for us to find is a pretty big mistake."

"Doctor Liu is the smart one. She's been playing Jake all the way."

Detective Abbott didn't like it. You don't find an exotic killing weapon at the suspect's house the day after personally telling him that he's a suspect. He'd seen white collar criminals make stupid mistakes but not like this. The evidence was a gift wrapped life sentence of premeditated murder. And it was pinned on the wrong suspect. "There's no way Jake Hawes did this on his own."

"What are you thinking?" Detective Delgado asked.

Abbott locked eyes with his partner. "We need to talk to Jake and only Jake for a long while. A whole day if needed. There's something missing. We've got to wear him down and get to the bottom of this."

"You don't put much stock in their patent chatter, do you?"

"No that's a Silicon Valley smoke screen."

"We've confirmed this weird love triangle. We have a solid motive." Detective Delgado pointed toward the RF generator. "Now we have the means."

"They worked with Amrish every day. There's no doubt they had opportunity."

"What's not to like about this case? It's practically gift wrapped with a bow on top."

"I was thinking the same thing and that's what I don't like about it." Detective Abbott was used to wrestling with evidence and teasing out motives. Abbott was used to seeing money rather than love as the prime motive for murder. Of course, the motive was more about revenge than love. There was another possibility. There was another reason for Jake to seek revenge. He turned to his partner. "What did Jake say when you told him he was about to be fired?"

"Nothing. He kept yapping about the patents."

"Could revenge for being fired be the motive? Perhaps Amrish was cutting him out of a big payday."

"That path gets messy. We'd be back on the patent red herring. Amrish was going to fire him to get him away from Doctor Liu."

"But we're sure he was about to be fired?"

"The REACT task force found the emails. They had an exit package all set up. Amrish was going to exit Jake the same day he was killed."

"A combination of revenge and love would make more sense. Jake and Doctor Liu knew he was about to get fired and Doctor Liu used that information to rope him into her murder scheme."

Detective Delgado nodded. "And she told him to take the button and RF generator out of her townhouse the night after Amrish's murder. Who knows about these technology guru types? Maybe Doctor Liu used extremely persuasive measures on him. You know – sex stuff."

"Yeah, I know." But he didn't. From what he saw of Doctor Jiao Liu, that seemed like a long shot. "It makes sense that she has a hold on him. But it can't be that strong a hold. We need to talk to Jake. We need him to turn on Doctor Liu."

"With all this evidence, why?"

"We're liable to prove beyond doubt that they were involved in the murder but not how. We go after them both and leave reasonable doubt that they did it alone. Or we go after Jake and miss because people realize he couldn't have done this. We'd have to prove Doctor Liu put Jake up to this." He looked at the RF generator and nodded. "We need to get Jake to turn on her."

"This button and RF box are evidence enough for arrests. We'll arrest Jake and Doctor Liu today. We'll separate them so they can be alone with their thoughts all night in a cell. Tomorrow, I'll work Jake all day long. I'll get him to turn on the good doctor."

Detective Abbott turned and looked at Jake's military medals gleaming in their shadowbox display. He felt uneasiness about their course of action but had no better idea. "Okay."

Detective Delgado pulled out his smartphone. "Our Palo Alto crew may have them by now." He punched a button on his phone and spoke into it. "You're in? Okay. I see." He lowered his phone and punched the hang-up button.

"What?"

"No one's in Doctor Liu's apartment."

"Did they find anything?"

"Nothing yet. They just got there. Doctor Liu's computer is gone and their cars aren't in the parking lot." Delgado grunted. "They're running."

"Maybe. Or maybe they're looking for something on their own." Abbott shook his head. "Where would they run?"

"I don't know but we better put an all points bulletin out on their plates. I'll also get the REACT guys to track their phones."

"Yes, do that. With phone tracking and cameras everywhere, they won't get far." Detective Abbott turned to Delgado. "We still should try to talk to Jake."

"How?"

"Send Jake a text message that you want to meet. Tell him you want to meet him alone for one last chance before the arrests put this whole thing in the legal system."

"Before we arrest them?"

"If we can get a hold of him."

"I'll try sending a text to his smartphone."

"Yeah, simply ask for confirmation that you can meet tomorrow for breakfast."

"Tomorrow?"

"Unless we pick them up tonight. They may not be in a cell yet but they'll be spinning all night anyway."

"Okay." Delgado scanned his phone. "There's a good breakfast place off Highway 101 on Ahwanee Avenue. I'll invite Jake to breakfast at Hobee's. It'll be neutral ground. We'll grab a booth and talk." Detective Delgado smiled. "I'll eat a big breakfast on the city's nickel and get Jake to turn on the good doctor. Are you going to join us?"

"No, he'll be more at ease with just you."

"Should I bring him in after breakfast?"

Abbott glanced around Jake's duplex. His gaze returned to the shadow box with eight military medals. He stared at the top medal – a bronze star with a 'v' device for valor. He nodded. "Yes, arrest him and bring him to the station. We'll detain him whether he turns on Doctor Liu or not."

"Why so glum?" Delgado pointed to the investigator crossing the room with the RF generator in an evidence bag. "This is cut and dried."

"I don't think so."

13

Jake was anxious upon leaving Jiao's townhouse but, the moment he merged on Highway 101 into stop-go traffic, he relaxed. The drive south was packed with cars, trucks, and SUVs of every size and description. Their phones were off and they were in bumper to bumper traffic. Police and fire truck lights flashed on both sides of the highway due to fender bender accidents. The three departed the townhouse with a minute between them and Jake had no sight of Hank or Jiao.

It's good, he thought. *It's good to hide in plain sight.* There were so many vehicles clogging the highway he figured the odds of them being picked up on this trip were remote. They would be found, there was no doubt about that, but Jiao was right. This move would buy them a precious day. They needed that day.

His automatic car lights flicked on as dusk approached. Jake rolled the events of the last forty-eight hours around in his mind. Amrish, the boss that was his friend and partner in their great renewable energy quest, betrayed him with Jiao. His great friend and partner not only betrayed him but did everything he could to alienate Jake the past few months. Jake was cut out of decision meetings and, just three days ago, was told he was being fired.

Jake remembered his rage. He had felt a surge of blind hate so strong he could have killed Amrish himself. And when the day to get fired came, Amrish was dead. When he first saw his old friend bleeding out on the floor, he felt justice was served. But what if he had it wrong? What if Amrish, by pushing him away, was trying to protect him? The button that killed him was no bush league weapon.

The button was set off remotely with something akin to RFID technology. The exploding button was a layered micro-capacitor triggered thin-film explosive device with microelectromechanical killer balls oriented to sever the carotid artery. That was crazy sophisticated technology. All this was packed in an innocuous shirt button. That killing button was technical marvel even the CIA would be proud to own.

Jake accelerated as the accordion traffic surged. Thirty seconds later he came to a complete stop. Just before he was murdered, Amrish sent Jiao a text about being in danger due to a patent, a philosopher's stone patent. According to Jiao, Amrish was pulling away from her as well. *Could it be*, Jake wondered, *that Amrish was trying to protect his friends? Protect Jiao and me?* It was a disturbing thought and Jake felt a pang of guilt remembering his 'karma is a bitch, justice is served' reaction upon finding Amrish face down on the floor of his office.

Two prime questions were left unanswered. Who would do this? Who had the power and the reach to do something like this? And why? Why would a patent lead to murder? They needed more information. Their enemies knew more about them than the police. The text he received made that clear. Jiao and Jake started searching the 221 patents and what happened? The police dismissed the patent search and their enemy threatened to kill again.

This evening, Jake thought as he pulled his red Camaro into the Residence Inn parking lot next to Jiao's BMW, *is all the time we have left to find out why. And finding out why is the only path.*

"What now?" Jake asked Jiao as he dropped his suitcase in the large Residence Inn suite. He noted both Hank and Jiao had gotten there ahead of him.

"I've got to go home," Hank said. "This threat has me rattled. I'm going to make sure my family's protected."

"We must find the answer," Jiao said. "The only way we protect ourselves is to find out why Amrish was murdered. We're the only ones who can solve this."

"What about the warning which talks about proof of our enemy's reach?" Hank asked.

"We brace to protect ourselves," Jake answered, "but I agree with Jiao. We have to find out why."

"We've got the night to think. That's it." Jiao spread her patent printouts out on the desk.

Hank nodded. "Do you want the burner phones and tablets?"

"Yes," Jake answered. "Just in case we have to leave in a hurry."

Hank departed for a few moments and returned with the Fry's Electronics bag. He handed it to Jake. "Good luck," Hank said at the door.

"Keep your head down," Jake said.

"You too."

Jake watched Hank depart and stared at the closed door. *Thank you Hank. You are a true friend.* He turned to Jiao. *Are you?* He didn't believe Detective Delgado's narrative but he didn't know what made Jiao tick. She was laser focused on any task but was an emotional stoic. Or she was until this murder. "How can I help?"

"I want to study all of these again. I downloaded all the 221 patent descriptions. I won't connect my laptop to Wi-Fi until early morning."

"Then we should keep our smartphones off until then as well."

"Yes."

"I see that focus I always loved about you."

Jiao's face lit and warmed the room. "Thank you. I have an idea I need to check."

"What is it?"

"Dan Brown's Da Vinci Code talked about finding the Holy Grail."

"You think this is like the Da Vinci Code mystery?"

"It's the idea of the search for the Holy Grail that got me thinking." She looked at Jake and cocked her head. "What is the Holy Grail of renewable energy that no one has been able to find?"

"The Holy Grail?" Jake pondered the last decade of California's and Silicon Valley's renewable energy fits and starts. "It's not grid parity cost at the solar module level. That was beat years ago."

"And it's not large solar farms that get sun all day. California has six or seven of the largest solar farms in the world but they still had to put in a dozen natural gas peak reactors in the major cities."

"Well that's because we use electricity as energy on demand. We have to be generating enough electricity at the moment we're using it. Otherwise you get the brownouts we all hate."

"That's why generating capacity has to be there for the peak demand which in California is 2:00 p.m. in August when all those air conditioners are going full blast."

"That's right. Even in December, with heaters on, the daily peak energy use is 20% lower than the dog days of August."

"You saw the same report we used for our DHS software algorithms. Do you remember what that report said about energy use over time during a day?"

"Sure. There's even a more dramatic swing than the seasonal variation. At 2:00 a.m. in the dog days of August California power use is over 40% less than at 2:00 p.m. That's why dream was always . . . holy cow!"

Jiao beamed. "Finish your thought."

"The dream was always energy storage. The Holy Grail of the next step in renewable energy is efficient energy storage." Jake walked over to Jiao. "That's brilliant. Efficient energy storage would negate the need for all these new installations. Everyone could store low cost energy off peak and use it when needed."

"We could reduce new energy generation needs by at least a third. If you add in storing the wasted wind turbine energy generated between midnight and 6:00 a.m. we could reduce new energy generation needs by half."

"Wind turbine energy?"

"That's the dirty little secret of all those wind turbines. There's no need for their nighttime generated electricity. They run that nighttime wind turbine generated electricity into load banks and dissipate it as heat." Jiao scowled. "They don't even capture and use the heat."

"If we could efficiently store all that wasted energy for when we need it . . ."

"We cut the need for additional sources in half. Can you imagine what a 50% cut in new energy generation needs would do?"

"That would threaten a lot of people."

"That's what I was thinking. An energy storage device would threaten people as powerful as the ones we're facing."

"I get it," Jake said. "That's what Amrish found."

"And it's somewhere in here. I'm going to set aside the desalination patents and everything else not connected to energy storage. Then I'm going to find the energy storage patent that scares our enemies so much."

14

The night wore on with coffee, energy drinks, and false starts. Of the 221 patents, 32 were related in some way to energy storage. Before departing Palo Alto, Jiao had printed out not just the patent description but also the claims and specifications. They looked for the devil in the details.

Jiao and Jake first went down the path of patent filings around the tried and true lead-acid battery. It seemed likely that companies like APC which supplied UPS – uninterruptable power sources – for computer systems would expand their lead-acid battery and inverter technology to accommodate home use. Amrish had three extensive patent filings around lead-acid batteries.

"This patent is based on thick plate lead-acid batteries that can handle deep cycles," Jake said.

"I see that," Jiao replied. "But look, I put together a cost spreadsheet on a power pack that would handle 30 kilowatt-hours in a 24 hour period."

"Why 30 kilowatt-hours?"

"According to the Department of Energy, the average American uses 901 kilowatt-hours per month. I used 30 kilowatt-hours as a proxy for a day's worth of energy for the storage unit."

"Does it work?"

Jiao shook her head. "It works but it's too expensive. The only ones who would make money on this scheme are the battery suppliers. Besides, expanding lead-acid battery production isn't environmental."

"Environmental concerns are the driving force for most renewable energy installations. No matter how much new technology we put into lead-acid batteries, it's a dead end."

Jiao looked at the displayed spreadsheet. "The Holy Grail of storage is not lead-acid batteries."

"I always liked fuel cells," Jake said. "They've been around since the space program and the byproduct of the hydrogen-oxygen fuel cells is pure water."

"There's a few of Amrish's energy storage patent filings on fuel cells. A couple are hydrogen-oxygen type similar to what NASA uses and a couple are solid oxide fuel cells like what Bloom Energy uses."

"Which has more promise?"

"It's a tradeoff. People are skittish about having compressed hydrogen tanks close by. Everyone remembers the Hindenburg. Solid oxide fuel cells generate a lot of heat, up to 800 degrees Celsius. That's why the use of both hydrogen-oxygen and solid oxide fuel cells is limited."

Jake liked mental intimacy of the patent search. They were trying to find an answer. Jake and Jiao were on a quest. It was a quest with high stakes and uncertain reward. But they were together. Jake reveled in the intimate closeness. "How about flow batteries?"

"There's three patents over there that cover flow batteries."

"I'll look at these while you're looking at the fuel cells."

Jiao shuffled papers and found the flow battery patents. She handed the sheaf of papers over and Jake clasped her hand with his left hand while his right grabbed the papers. He looked in her eyes. "Do you trust me now?"

She nodded. "I do but if we don't find it . . ."

"I know." Jake dropped her hand and swiveled to the patents. "It's odd how all of Amrish's filings are apparatus or process tweaks of older patents."

"Well, remember how Apple patented the specific curve of the case of their Macbooks?"

"Amrish's patents are like that?"

"It seems so. Most of what he filed are new applications of existing technology – prior art."

"Then why file? It only highlights information that's already public. Remember how we'd never file for patents on our most closely guarded ideas? Without the publication of the patent award, we could better protect our trade secrets. Why would Amrish patent all these tweaks to existing technology?"

"I was with Amrish until last month and I wasn't aware he was doing any of this."

Jake reacted to the 'with Amrish' comment as if he'd been slapped in the face. He swallowed. "Do you trust me as much as you trusted Amrish?"

Jiao turned from her papers. "It doesn't work like that Jake. Trust takes time."

"We don't have much time Jiao."

She nodded. "And trust takes commitment. I do see your commitment."

"Good." He turned back to the flow battery patents. As he read Jake became convinced that flow batteries were another dead end. "The problem with these flow battery patent filings is low voltage. These electrochemical batteries take large tanks of chemicals, an unreliable membrane, and only produce 1.2 volts. Do you think these could be scaled?"

"To be cost effective? I don't think so." Jiao tapped her stack of patents. "These fuel cells are reversible, which is important, but are too expensive. Even the solid oxide fuel cell here that uses natural gas as a source like Bloom Energy is just too expensive. Fuel cells don't look cost effective."

"What if everyone was fine with storing compressed hydrogen in a closet?"

"Even then," Jiao answered, "the cost is prohibitive. These work for NASA because they have to have them. Cost is no object when you die without them."

"You think fuel cells are a dead end?"

"I'm still looking."

"I'm going to look at the lithium-ion and rechargeable alkaline power pack patents. I don't think flow batteries are viable."

"Read carefully," Liao said. "We only have tonight."

"Yes, we only have tonight for this quest."

"Then we may be separated for life."

Jake was jarred by the blunt statement. "No, we're going to find the answer."

"It's been five hours. We could turn our phones on for a quick email download."

Jake nodded. "When we turn on our phones it'll be like popping a flare for the police to see. It needs to be a quick on and off." He looked at Jiao. "Do you think it's worth the risk to turn our phones on?"

Jiao nodded. "We should get one more download of our communications. Hank may have sent something. The police may have sent something."

"I'm sure the police sent something. They probably emailed us that we're under arrest and need to turn ourselves in or a SWAT team is going to show up." He looked at his watch. "It's 3:00 a.m. Let's wait another hour before popping that flare."

"This will be the last chance. After this, we run. When we run, we'll take the burner phones and tablets and leave our regular smartphones here." She stared at the screen. "I'll have to leave this laptop as well."

"Let's get ready to run before turning our phones on."

"I don't know where to run to."

"I have an idea."

"Where?"

"Hiding in plain sight."

They used the hour to plumb the depths of other patent filings but none seemed promising. "This static electricity generator is interesting," Jiao said. "You can get power on a daily basis."

"Could that be the technology that scares someone?"

Jiao frowned. "I don't think so. The power is inconsistent and at such low level, you couldn't build a big enough device."

"No luck from my search either." He looked at his watch. "It's 4:00 a.m."

"Okay, we'll do this quick. Let's turn on our smartphones and I'll connect to the Residence Inn Wi-Fi."

The two, bleary-eyed and disheveled, turned on their smartphones. Both devices beeped as their phones updated. Jake blinked at one of the messages. "Whoa!"

"What?"

"Lemme open it. I got a text from Detective Delgado."

"Really?"

Jake tapped the message icon and scrolled down. "Hmmm. He wants to meet me for breakfast at 7:00 a.m. to cover recent evidence."

"Just you?"

"Yes, he's specific about that. He says he'll be alone but only meet if I come alone." He exhaled. "Fine then. I'll tell him I'm not going without you." Jake tapped his phone.

"Wait," Jiao said. "Wait. If he wants to meet you, he's found something."

"But if he wants to meet only me, he wants me to turn on you."

Jiao was silent for a long moment. "You asked if I trust you." She nodded. "I do. I do trust you. Go and meet him for breakfast."

"What if he arrests me?"

"Then I'll search for the patent on my own. We have to get that answer but Jake, we also have new information. Share that with the detective."

"What new information?"

"Tell Detective Delgado the patent is about energy storage. Tell him that's the only thing that could scare high powered enemies."

"Do you think he'll believe me?"

"It's worth a try."

Jake rose and shuddered. "I could sleep for a week."

"No time for that now." Jiao looked at her smartphone. "Hank is going to be here at 8:00 a.m."

"I was copied on that message too."

"Go to breakfast . . . if they were going to arrest us, he wouldn't have asked to meet only you."

Jake didn't like that comment. He felt they were being played. The police could arrest them anytime they wanted.

"Where does he want to meet you?"

"In a public place – at Hobee's off of Ahwanee Avenue."

"They have great breakfasts there."

"Are you sure it's a good idea for me to go?"

"I'm not sure but do it anyway."

"Okay. At least I'll get to eat."

15

Jake walked into the Sunnyvale Hobee's at 6:45 a.m. The parking lot, as near as he could tell, was free of police cars. He noticed Detective Delgado sitting in a booth in the corner. He glanced around and saw no one near the detective. "Jake, over here." Delgado waved to him.

Jake went down the aisle and sat across from the detective. He was able to see the exit door to his left and positioned himself for a quick dash.

"Relax," Detective Delgado said. "If I wanted to arrest you, you'd be in handcuffs by now. Let's have a nice breakfast courtesy of the city budget."

Jake faced the detective. He was wary that the good cop façade would drop in a moment. "What are we going to talk about?"

Before Detective Delgado could answer the server came to their booth. "Coffee?"

"Yes please," Delgado answered.

Jake flipped his cup over. "Me too."

The server filled their cups. "I'll be back in a minute to take your orders."

"Thank you," Delgado said.

"Your text said you had more information."

The detective nodded. "We do. First, do you have anything more to add?"

Jake hated this cat and mouse game. "Yes, but you first. What new information did you find?"

"It might be better if you go first."

Jake narrowed his eyes. "You have it all wrong. We are honing in on the patent that got Amrish killed."

"Murdered. Amrish was murdered."

The server came back. "Did you guys decide?"

Jake glanced down at the breakfast section of the menu. "I'll have the Stanford 'Cardinal' Omelet and some orange juice."

The detective laughed. "Hungry eh? You must've had a light dinner." He turned to the server. "Just a toasted bagel for me."

"Right away sir." The server departed.

Jake drank half of his coffee down in one gulp. He relished the warmth as it spread through him. Jake and Jiao had found the answer to why Amrish was killed. That had to be something. This was big news and there was no way the police figured it out yet. Jake locked eyes with Delgado. "Amrish was murdered to stop an energy storage device from getting out there."

The detective laughed out loud. "Are you kidding me? That's what you've come up with?"

"Think about it. The energy use delta from peak to trough is 40%. If you could store energy at low use times, there wouldn't be an energy problem. There wouldn't be a climate problem. Amrish filed a patent for an energy storage device. It's the Holy Grail of renewable energy."

"Quit screwing around." Detective Delgado leaned over the table and moved his face into Jake's personal space. "We found your girlfriend's button and trigger at your duplex yesterday."

"Trigger?"

"Yeah, it was some box our techs say will pop the button like what happened to your boss."

"You found this at my place?"

"You look surprised."

"You think I'd be so stupid as to leave a button and trigger in my duplex for you to find?"

"We think your girlfriend, Doctor Jiao Liu, is quite persuasive."

Jake let the comment hang in the air. This breakfast was a mistake. Delgado didn't bat an eye at the energy storage conclusion. The police were locked on the love triangle motive. Jake wondered if Delgado would even entertain an alternate theory. "Detective, I want you to consider something."

"What's that?"

"What if you're wrong? What if I have nothing to do with this? What if Jiao has nothing to do with this? Ask yourself. If we don't have anything to do with it, who does? Who has the power and reach to do something like this? The answer to that question will put us both on the right track."

"Saying you've been framed won't work. That's too crazy a leap. We found the murder weapon in your duplex. We know Amrish was about to fire you. We know you and Doctor Jiao Liu are in a romantic relationship." The detective opened his hands in a palms up expression indicating it was crazy to think different.

"That's not . . ."

"We know only you and your girlfriend had motive, means, and opportunity. The only thing we don't know is if Doctor Liu played you. If she did, you should tell me – right now. After the prosecutor gets involved, it'll be too late. That's what this breakfast is about."

Jake felt a sheen of sweat form on his forehead. His cheeks burned and he knew his face was beet red. Jake's racing thoughts ground to a crawl. He swallowed. "Wait. Let me show you something." He pulled his smartphone out of his pocket and punched the messages button. He scanned until he found the threatening text. Jake handed his smartphone to Delgado.

"What's this?" The detective read the message out loud. "Jake – stop looking for answer to Amrish's death or Jiao and Hank will die. We will save you from jail and provide proof of our reach." He laughed. "See that's all wrong because after our nice breakfast, you are going to be in jail."

Jake's jaw unhinged. "This was a mistake."

"Here's your Stanford 'Cardinal' Omelet, sir." The server set the brimming plate in front of Jake. "And here's your toasted bagel." She set a plate in front of Detective Delgado. "I'll be right back to top off your coffee."

"Enjoy your breakfast Jake. That's the last decent food you're going to have for a long time."

Jake wanted to say more but the server returned and topped off their coffee. He wanted his smartphone back but the detective kept it beside him on the table.

Detective Delgado carefully cut his bagel in two and coated each half with cream cheese. He took a bite. "Mmm . . . good." Delgado was enjoying himself. He took a sip of coffee. "You have only one play here. Your only play is to turn on your girlfriend."

Jake stirred the events over and over in his mind. He still had doubts about Jiao's true feelings but he knew for a fact she wasn't the murderer. He knew for a fact she never went to his duplex. Whoever planted an exploding button and trigger in his duplex did so after he got his clothes two days ago.

"Eat Jake. You'll regret it later if you don't."

He forked off a corner of the omelet and put it in his mouth. The omelet's tomatillo sauce aroma made his mouth water but the food tasted like chewing wet newspaper. Jake forced a swallow. The food hung in his throat. He took a sip of coffee and washed it down. "That text . . ."

"Means absolutely nothing." Detective Delgado took a large bite of his toasted bagel and grinned as he chewed.

Jake stared at the smug detective and felt a surge of hate. *Destroying us is sport to you.* What was worse, the unknown powerful enemy was still out there. Jake looked down at his omelet. His ears started ringing. He frowned and lifted his head. Detective Delgado swallowed and lifted his coffee cup. A sharp pop sounded across the table. The detective lowered his coffee cup with a startled expression. "What did you . . ."

Jake saw it. First a trickle and then a spurt of blood. His eyes widened as Delgado slapped his hand to his neck. The detective's blood oozed past his fingers and spread into a wide cone on the front of his shirt. Jake was frozen in panic.

Detective Delgado gurgled and uttered something but only blood-spattered breath escaped his mouth. He grappled for his gun and then grabbed his neck with his second hand. His face, once flushed with color, turned pale white.

Jake's panic broke. He surged forward and grabbed his smartphone. He slid out of the booth and took the shortest distance to the door. He popped out of the building and heard a 'wait' as the door closed behind him. He ran across the parking lot, got into his Camaro, and started it. He zoomed out of the parking lot just as a server ran out of the building heading his direction.

He merged on Highway 101 and exhaled. *Did that just happen?* He saw blood spots on his forearm that erased his doubt. His mind was locked onto one question. *Who? Who is doing this to us? Who could do this?*

16

Hank looked around the Residence Inn Suite and noted that a blanket was draped on the couch. He frowned.

"We didn't share a bed," Jiao said. "Jake napped there." Jiao pointed to the couch. "And I used the bed."

Hank nodded. "Where is Jake?"

"He left to meet with Detective Delgado at seven to tell him what we found."

Hank looked at his watch. "It's 8:05 now. I hope Jake's not in handcuffs."

Jiao went to the suite's kitchen. "They have coffee packets here. Do you want a cup?"

"Sure, if you don't need it."

"I drink tea." Jiao pulled a coffee mug out of the cupboard and filled the small brewer with water. She popped in a coffee cartridge and pushed the brew button.

Hank found the domesticity disconcerting. "Tell me what you found."

"We didn't find it yet but we know what it is."

"Okay, what is it?"

"The Holy Grail of renewable energy."

"The Holy Grail?" Hank frowned and then raised his eyebrows. "You mean storage?"

"Yes. Amrish found an energy storage technology."

"But you don't know what it is?"

"Not yet."

"Everyone in renewable energy has been looking for efficient storage for the last twenty years."

Jiao handed him a steaming cup of coffee. "Is black okay?"

"Black is perfect." Hank took the cup and blew on it. "The best storage device by far is massive amounts of water collected above a turbine. Nothing beats the Hoover Dam or San Luis Reservoir concept and that type of energy storage is geographically limited."

"Amrish found something else."

"How do you know?"

Both turned at a thumping sound on the front door. Jake burst into the suite, wide eyed and out of breath. "They killed him."

Hank set his coffee down and went to Jake. "What happened?"

"Detective Delgado . . . we were eating breakfast . . . he didn't believe me . . . his button exploded."

"You mean the detective was killed? In front of you?"

Jake lifted his forearm and showed the blood spots. "I was sitting right across from him."

Jiao stepped forward. "What did you do after the button went off?"

"I got out of there as fast as I could." He looked at Jiao. "They found an exploding button and trigger in my duplex yesterday. We're being framed." He took two deep breaths. "Detective Delgado was going to arrest me right there in Hobee's."

"That doesn't make sense. If he was going to arrest you and you were framed, why kill him?"

"I don't know. We have to go." He looked up. "Jiao get your stuff together. We have to go and go now."

Jiao bounded up the stairs and started putting bundles of paper in a satchel. "Where? Where can we go?"

"I could take you to my place in South Lake Tahoe," Hank said. "That was the option I planned to offer when I came here."

"Too far," Jake said. "If we go that far, we'll never be able to come back."

"You said you have an idea to hide in plain sight," Jiao said as she packed her toiletries.

Jake opened his carryon suitcase and took the suite's blankets. He unzipped the expansion to accommodate the blankets and forced it closed. "We hide in plain sight right next to Fry's."

"What are you talking about?" Hank asked.

"There's an ugly white and blue glass office building behind the Shell station on Lawrence and Arques. I know someone who worked at the software company that leased it. They went out of business and left three weeks ago."

"You want to hide in a vacant office building in Sunnyvale?"

"I saw it when we drove by and got the idea. They disconnected the security cameras and just left it. I saw lights on when we drove by to get our burner phones. It has power."

Jiao came downstairs with her satchel and suitcase. "I left my smartphone and laptop upstairs. Whomever we're up against knew you were meeting Detective Delgado this morning and managed to get an exploding button on his shirt."

"And set it off just as he was about to arrest me." Jake shook his head. He pulled his smartphone from his pocket and set it on the counter. He opened the closet and extracted the Fry's bag with their burner phones. He turned to Hank. "Can you drive us there? Our cars will give us away."

Hank nodded. "Let's go."

Jiao and Jake piled into Hank's Mustang. "Damn, this is smaller than my Camaro," Jake said.

"And faster."

Hank drove the few blocks from the Residence Inn to the newly vacant office building behind the Arques Shell station. He pulled his Mustang around the back and noted that the parking lot was empty but adjacent to one with a few cars.

"Those parked cars are for the building next door," Jake said. "These new office buildings have a poor track record for keeping businesses."

The three got out. Hank popped open the trunk and Jake and Jiao grabbed their suitcases, satchel, and Fry's bag. Jake jogged to the back door. He pulled a card from his wallet, put it in the door latch, and popped it open.

"You're lucky they didn't keep those magnetic locks activated." Hank held the door.

Jiao and Jake hustled inside. Jake turned to his friend. "I have to ask one more favor."

"What?"

"We need food and sleeping bags. Can you help?"

Hank went inside the building. "I can. What food works?"

"My friend said the breakroom was left alone. Let's see if it has a microwave." The three went around the corner and were elated to find a breakroom with microwave and refrigerator.

"I'm beginning to see the virtue of this hiding place."

"You ought to get your car away from here since it's daytime."

"I'll be back at midnight, sharp."

Hank jogged to the door and left. Jake and Jiao stared at each other as they heard the throaty V-8 in Hank's Mustang rev. They heard the dimming sound of their one friend drive away. As the distinctive rumble died down an eerie quiet settled over the building.

Jiao looked at Jake. "Are you okay?"

"I don't know. I have to think. From the moment I sat down with Detective Delgado my thoughts have been gummed up."

"What did he say before the button . . ."

Jake and Jiao walked to the door. Jake closed it until he heard a satisfying click. "He thought we did it." Jake cleared his throat. "They found a button and trigger in my apartment yesterday."

"You said that when you came into the suite." Jiao nodded. "You said he was going to arrest you."

"He gave me one last chance to turn on you but yes, he was going to arrest me . . . right after breakfast. And then his button blew those barbed balls into his neck."

The two took their bags and suitcases and moved away from the glass wall. They found a large empty room in the middle of the building. "This must've been a conference room." Jake closed the door and pulled the blinds. The room was pitch black save for a red LED glint at the light switch. "Let's see if the lights work."

Jiao tapped the light button and both were suffused in a harsh florescent glow. "Not very feng shui but it'll work." She put her back to the wall and slowly sank to the floor. "But why Jake? Our enemies had the perfect frame going. Why kill the detective?"

"It was like their text said. They saved us from jail and demonstrated their reach." Jake sat next to Jiao on the floor of the empty room. "They put us in an impossible position."

"But why?"

"They want us to run." Jake tried to push the horror of the detective's murder from his mind. "Think about their power. They got an exploding button on the detective's shirt and set it off in front of me."

Jiao turned to Jake. "That means they're everywhere and they know everything."

"They're watching our every move."

Jiao tapped the satchel of papers. "The answer has to be in here. I looked at every patent twice. For a while I thought it must be flow batteries. There's new ideas around that technology but nothing's cost effective."

"We've been looking at patents ever since Amrish's murder because of that odd philosopher's stone text. We looked all last night when we were at the Residence Inn."

"We're missing something."

"I can't go through these again." Jake shook his head. "Not now anyway. I just hear that pop and see the blood spurt from Delgado's neck. Who has that kind of reach?"

Jiao stared at the wall. "And do they know we're here?"

17

"Dear, what was killing the detective meant to achieve?" Arjun lowered the paper. In this digital age Arjun still liked the old fashioned habit of the daily newspaper. He gazed at his wife.

"We had to raise the stakes," Lalita replied.

"The news published wanted pictures of Jake Hawes and Jiao Liu. They're calling for their arrest in connection with two murders. Is that what you intended?"

"Those two are on everyone's mind now."

"But we lost track of them. For the first time since Amrish's death, we don't know where they are."

"That's not a bad thing. They left behind their smartphones and cars. Whatever they're doing, they can't be searching for the magic patent."

"There's nothing magic about it. That's the problem." Arjun crossed the room and encircled his wife's waist from behind. "What did you want? Did you want them to flee or to be jailed for life?"

"I want them to die. The police will leave no stone unturned."

"But we've lost visibility. There's a lot of uncertainty in how this will unfold."

Lalita turned and smiled. "Detective Abbott is dedicating half of the police force to find them."

"But they're not armed. Why would the police kill them?"

"If they get arrested, we'll deal with them in jail. And don't forget, there're more buttons out there dear."

"Ah yes, the unaccounted for buttons. I doubt we'll be able to use that trick again."

"Did the news mention it?"

"No, they haven't disclosed how Amrish or Detective Delgado were killed."

"Then the trick will work again."

Arjun crossed the room and slid into the leather padded chair behind his desk. "This is distracting us. There's no guarantee someone else won't stumble on the energy technology. If someone like Amrish can find it, others can. After this investigation dies down, we need to co-opt the patent. We need to control it."

Lalita shook her head. "The United States Department of Energy will have something to say about that."

Arjun looked across the room at the book lined shelves, recognition plaques, and pictures of state politicians. The political pictures had one thing in common – the politician stood in the center with Arjun on their right and Lalita on their left. The couple always flanked the politician they planned to influence. He looked at Lalita. "You're right. We don't deal in technology. We'll leave that to others."

"That's why we're winning."

"We are so close. Our subsidiaries cover every piece of the legislated renewable energy market." He chuckled. "Renewable energy. Solar inverters get scrapped after eight years and after twenty years, solar panels lose their ability to generate electricity. They become nothing more than worthless hunks of hazardous waste."

"As that happens all of our subsidiaries' reclamation government contracts double our take. We'll be reinstalling the solar farms and reclaiming them at the same time. It's just like our inverter replacements now, we make money with every installation and every maintenance replacement."

"You know our reclamation business doesn't meet the government specification. We may be fined for improper disposal."

"We've discussed this dear. The money we make will far exceed the fines we might pay. It's the right tradeoff."

"All those political contributions are good for something."

"They're a good investment. Everyone trades in favors. The fault's in those who don't admit it."

Arjun smiled at his wife. "You have a backbone of steel." He turned and looked out the window at the rolling brown hills. Before the back to back droughts he remembered those hills being green in the spring and gold in the summer. They didn't look gold now. "Amrish . . . who would have thought someone like Amrish would be the one to find that patent."

"It had to be Amrish. Silicon Valley thrives on the new. That's why Jake and Jiao searched for two days and found nothing."

"We don't know that. They may be sending device designs around the country right now. That would destroy our future."

"They're running, they're hunted, and they're scared. I'd never want to be in their shoes."

"With the game we're playing dear, this could turn on us. The patent must remain hidden. At least until we're ready to use it."

"That's why Detective Delgado had to die in front of Jake. Emotion's as big a shield for us as secrecy."

"We don't know where Jake and Jiao are. We don't know what they're doing. Maybe they're running. Maybe they're a thousand miles away in the Mexican sun."

"Did their friend Hank disappear?"

"No, he showed up for work today like usual. We'll keep an eye on him."

"Credit card swipes, buses, trains, flights . . . Jake and Jiao must show up somewhere."

"Their last credit card swipe was yesterday at the Sunnyvale Residence Inn. After that, we see nothing. They've abandoned their cars, a laptop, and their phones." He looked at his wife. "It was the Detective's death that caused their disappearance."

"I'll get my man on it."

"You mean your brother Laksh."

"Yes."

"What about the other buttons?"

"Leave those to me dear."

Lalita was concerned. Her aura of detachment and control was for Arjun. Their past power moves, up to and including murder, were always discreet and over in quick fashion. This problem was dragging on in time and expanding in scope. The news called attention to Jake and Jiao but there was danger someone would look past the love triangle. She had to mitigate that danger.

She dove her Bentley home to their palatial Los Altos Hills estate and parked in the warehouse size garage full of antique and exotic cars. She walked from the garage and went straight to their guest house. She entered without knocking.

"Ah, my beauty pageant sister returns," Laksh said. "I see from the news that Detective Delgado and Jake Hawes didn't enjoy their morning breakfast. That's so sad. Breakfast is the most important meal of the day."

"Do you know where Jake and Jiao are?"

"No but the police are on high alert. With all the security cameras and electronic payment monitoring, they're bound to turn up soon."

"Someone is helping them."

"We know Hank Rudzinski is helping them. He was in the army with Jake."

"Did he do anything unusual?"

"Not that we've seen. But we're still looking." Laksh motioned to the couch. "Didi, sweet Didi . . . you are worried."

"You have not called me that since I was a child dear brother."

"That was the last time I saw you scared. For all that we have been through and all we have done to stake our claim, this is just another step."

Lalita reached back and popped one heeled shoe off and then the other. "I'll sit for a moment." She glided barefoot to the couch, sat, and pulled her legs under her. "It may have been a mistake to kill the detective."

"No. That has put all the focus on Jake and Jiao. No one is looking elsewhere. And no one will."

"How does this resolve?"

"As we discussed, jail or death."

"Jail doesn't work. If they are alive, they will enlist more help to search for patents. That's the last thing we want."

"If they get jailed, they'll be dead soon after. Is that why you're here Didi? You want me to guarantee their deaths?"

Lalita looked away for a moment and then turned back to Laksh. "That's the only way to be sure."

"Family, future, and fortune – this should secure it all. Didn't we toast to that last New Year's?" Laksh sat next to his sister and hugged her. "And then this happens."

"Family, future, and fortune – those are the only things that matter."

"Then we do whatever it takes to ensure Jake and Jiao's death. There're no moral or legal bounds save one."

"Yes, don't get caught."

18

Jake waited and watched the back door of the vacant office building as the clock approached midnight. *Hank will be here soon.* He replayed the previous days over and over again in his mind in hopes of making sense of their position. If the killer would've waited a week, Jake would've been fired and out of the loop. Perhaps that's what Amrish intended.

Amrish knew he was in trouble. He texted that in clear terms to Jiao the night before he was murdered. But Detective Delgado had no idea he was in danger. Delgado even knew an exploding button killed Amrish but never considered that he would suffer the same fate.

Betrayal, murders, and a real love triangle were involved – but for what? Jake shivered and stared at the dark parking lot. What patent – which was a public document anyway – so upset the status quo to cause this mayhem? He and Jiao had to be right. It had to be a storage patent and they had to find it.

Jake looked behind him. Jiao was in the conference room, wrapped in the Residence Inn blankets, and dozing. They had shelter, water, and would soon have food. But the isolation since abandoning their smartphones was total. Jake didn't even know if Delgado survived. There must've been a chance that he lived. Maybe he lived and could help clear this up.

A tan colored van without headlights drove into the parking lot. Jake's heart pounded until he saw the familiar silhouette of Hank Rudzinski bound out and jog toward the door. Jake popped the door open as Hank approached. "Where'd you get the van?"

"It's a leased delivery van we're using to move office equipment around. I didn't want to bring my car back here." Hank was all business. "Besides, I couldn't fit all this gear in my Mustang."

Jiao appeared around the corner. "Hey Hank, did you bring us enough to live on?"

"I brought enough for you guys to hole up for a week or two if you could stand it." Let's get the van unpacked.

Hank wasn't kidding. He procured two weeks' worth of microwave dinners as well as Costco sized containers of milk, cereal, paper plates, plastic cups, plastic utensils and cases of soup. He provided two sleeping bags, soap, and washcloths. He even thought of paper towels and garbage bags. The three put the food in the break room and the rest of the supplies in their conference room.

"This room is nicely nestled in the middle of the building," Hank said as Jiao turned on the light. Hank opened his briefcase and pulled out a copy of the Mercury News. He extended it to Jake. "Whatever you two need to find, you need to find it fast. The news published pictures of you both in connection to Amrish's and Detective Delgado's murder."

Jake looked at the paper. "So he did die." He read further and gasped. "They have a countywide manhunt for us?"

Jiao came alongside Jake and read the paper. "The police think you killed Delgado."

"There's a write up in there of the love triangle between you two and Amrish." Hank pulled four yellow legal pads out of his briefcase and set them on the conference room floor. He tossed a packet of pens and a packet of pencils on top the legal pads. The last thing he pulled out was a paper Bay Area map. He tossed the map on top of the pens. "It looks like you guys are going to be old school for a while. These might help."

"They will, thanks." Jake picked up one of the pen packages.

Hank pointed to the map. "If you go anywhere, you better go at night and avoid anyplace that has cameras."

Jake picked up the map. "A legal pad and a paper map. This is old school."

Hank looked from one to the other. "I stuck my neck out as far as I can guys." He looked at Jake. "You remember what they always said about going through a minefield."

"Sure," Jake answered. He pulled a pen from the package and picked up a legal pad. "You never put more into harm's way than you have to. You were the hero leading the convoy through the minefield in Iraq Hank. This is my minefield."

Hank nodded. "I'll leave you to it. The only way you get me back is to use one of those four burner phones we got at Fry's."

"I understand," Jake said as the three walked from the conference room to the door. He extended a hand to his friend. "I've got to go through this minefield alone."

"Not alone," Jiao said. She hugged Hank. "Thank you."

"Good luck."

The vacant building was quiet after Hank left. Jake and Jiao stared at the door a long moment after the van disappeared. Jake went to the door and ensured it was latched. He turned and saw Jiao pick up two rolled sleeping bags. "Good idea."

The two walked into the conference room and laid out the bags on opposite sides. Jake lay his legal pad and pen in front of his bag. "I need to organize my thoughts."

Jiao looked up smiled. "Let's eat something first."

Hank furnished them with a mix of western and Asian microwave dinners. The microwave could only cook one at a time and the only setting was high. Jiao cooked her Yakisoba Noodles meal first and Jake popped in the tried and true Salisbury steak with gravy and mashed potatoes. As his meal was heating he heard a chuckle from Jiao. He turned. "What?"

"Hank even remembered chop sticks."

"We owe him for this. No matter what happens to us, he's liable to be pulled in."

"He was careful."

The microwave beeped and Jake extracted his meal. The aroma of the processed meal made him salivate. "I am hungry." He turned and felt a pang seeing Jiao waiting for him before eating herself.

"We should get away from the glass door." The two took their meals and plastic cups filled with water and went to their conference room. Jake sat on the floor.

Jiao set her container of steaming noodles and cup of water on the floor. She disappeared for a moment and returned with two chairs. "It might be easier to eat sitting in a chair."

"Good call." Jake sat next to Jiao in a chair and pulled the plastic off his meal. He cut a piece of the ground beef and popped it in his mouth. "Mmm . . . I am so hungry." He saw Jiao was eating her noodles with relish. "I see you were too."

"We need food. I can't think on an empty stomach."

Jake cut a second piece of his steak and scooped a large dollop of mashed potatoes with it. He dipped it in the processed gravy and put it in his mouth. He felt rejuvenating energy by simply chewing the food. He swallowed. "I never thought a microwave dinner would make me tear up in gratitude." Jiao chuckled and it sounded like music.

"I never ate microwave noodles before."

"Really?"

"We always had the hot water dispenser on the coffee machine at work." She used her chopsticks to take another bite. "I never knew what I was missing." She smiled and wiped her chin with a napkin. She noticed Jake didn't have any napkins. She set her chopsticks in the cardboard noodle bowl, lifted a napkin from the stack on her knee, and extended it to Jake.

Jake took the napkin. "Thank you. Good noodles, huh?"

"Great noodles." Jiao went back to work with her chopsticks.

He laughed. "You're pretty cool Jiao, you really are."

Jiao stopped her noodle bundle halfway to her mouth and beamed at Jake. Her eyes shone. "So are you Jake. I'm sorry I mixed you up in this."

"I'm not." He leaned toward her until their shoulders were touching. "No matter how screwed up this is, I'm glad to be next to you."

Jiao leaned into him and smiled. "Thank you Jake."

"I'm sorry about that throughput thing. I never stopped trusting you." He shook his head. "You always are the pillar of the strong independent woman. I didn't think it was big deal."

"You think I'm strong?"

"You're one of the strongest people I know."

Jiao shook her head. "I'm not. I work like I do because I'm lonely. After my husband Keng died and then my daughter left." She sighed and shuddered. "I'm so lonely. That's why I needed Amrish."

Jake saw his comments about throughput a year ago in a different light. Jiao poured everything into the Urban Solar customer opportunity and, the person she wanted to trust most in the world, publically criticized her. He inhaled. He chanced draping his arm across her shoulders. She leaned into him. "I'll be your companion," Jake said. "You don't need to be lonely again."

They finished their meals. Both drank their water. Jake rose and took Jiao's cup. "I'll refill these."

Jiao got up. "We must top off our dinner. I saw that Hank remembered to get green tea."

Jake followed her into the breakroom and filled the two cups with water. "Tea?"

"Tea." Jiao microwaved water in a plastic bowl, poured it into two double plastic cups, and brewed green tea. She turned and handed a cup to Jake. "This will settle everything and help us think."

"Thank you." Jake handed a cup of water to Jiao. The two returned to the conference room, each carrying two cups.

Jake sat next to Jiao again on the chair. He set his water beside him and took a sip of green tea. The light sweet taste with an earthy undertone was the right cap to his meal. He smiled. "This is perfect . . . better than our few dinner dates."

Jiao returned the smile. "Yes." She turned and looked at the semi-organized stacks of papers. "At least we have this moment."

They drank their tea and water shoulder to shoulder. Jake felt peace listening to nothing more than the sound of their breaths. The quiet felt good after the nonstop reaction since the murder. Jake looked at the stack of papers. "We have to get ahead of this."

"Hmm?"

"We're reacting. Somehow we have to find out what's driving this."

"I went through every storage patent twice last night. I looked at all the others as well. I need rest first."

"Me too," Jake said. Jiao arose and Jake shuddered at the loss of her warmth. "It's been a nonstop three days." He stood, regretful the intimate moment passed. "I'm glad the bathrooms have water."

Jiao was also thinking about the bathrooms. She pulled out her toiletries. "I'm going to wash."

Jake followed suit. He went to the men's room, brushed his teeth, and performed the wet rag wash he did so often as an officer in the U.S. Army. He even shaved with his electric razor. He didn't know why that was important but it felt good. He returned to the conference room and saw that Jiao was already in her sleeping bag. He lay his toiletries on top of his suitcase and turned off the light.

"Good night Jake," Jiao said.

"Good night." Jake stripped to his underwear and slid into his sleeping bag. The hard floor and cool bag chilled him but in moments fatigue took over and he dozed.

A light wail from Jiao awoke him. He snapped upright and listened. He could just make out her outline from the red LED light. He listened and heard her sobbing. "Hey, Jiao . . . what's the matter?"

"I'm cold."

Jake got out of his sleeping bag and shivered. "Whoa. It is cold." He pulled his sleeping bag next to Jiao's. "We can zip the two bags together. I'll keep you warm." Their situation was raw. He hoped she'd accept the idea. He wanted to comfort as much as warm this lonely woman.

She turned, eyes shining. "Okay."

It took some doing to get the two zippers lined up in the dark but Jake persisted. He managed to get the two sleeping bags zipped together into one big one. He held the opening. "Get in. I'll get you warm."

Jiao slid into the bag and Jake was acutely aware that she had also stripped and was wearing nothing but a t-shirt and panties. Even in the near pitch black, seeing the always precisely dressed woman in that attire sent a jolt through Jake. He slid in beside her. "Come here."

Jiao, without the slightest hesitation, moved into an embrace with Jake. She put her head on his shoulder, wrapped her arms around him, and slung a bare leg over his thighs.

Jake's heart was about to burst. He wrapped both arms around her shoulders and hugged her close. "I got you. You're okay now."

"Thank you Jake. Thank you."

For three peaceful hours the two lay in their embrace. Jake didn't know if he dozed during that time. He was in Jiao's warm clasp and that was enough. He gave her his warmth and found strength. Their communion, borne of this unexpected threat, wiped out past misunderstandings. They welded together in union against evil. Jake hugged this woman and wished above all else to always keep her warm, to always protect her.

Jiao stirred awake at 3:55 a.m. She pulled back from Jake, disoriented. She took a deep breath and then wrapped Jake in firm hug. "Oh, I'm glad you're here."

Jake returned the embrace. "I'm not leaving you." He felt Jiao's hand trace the outside of his shoulder. "Mmm, nice." Her hand slid down to his hip. Jake pulled his head back and, in the dim light, stared into her eyes. He slipped his hand behind her head and descended into a kiss of no more than brushed lips.

She lifted her head and the two kissed in earnest. He felt her tug his underwear down. He pulled back and noted that her eyes were shining. "Very nice."

They kissed again, mingling tongues and releasing pent passion. Jake slid his hand to her hip, found the elastic of her panties, and tugged. She lifted her hips and he slid her panties off. He cradled her in one arm and rolled over her. She used that movement to slide his underwear down and then grasped him.

He used his elbows to keep most of his weight off of her. She put him inside and wrapped her legs around his waist. He felt ease and completeness in the encirclement. She pulled his head to hers and dug her nails into his back. Their coupling completed the warm intimacy of their nighttime embrace. Their yearning movements were slow and deliberate. Jake wanted the moment to last an eternity. He would never let her go. Never.

The two stretched the moment of their physical communion and arousal. They communicated their trust and love without saying a word. The couple united their bodies, their passions, and their spirits. They were one. Their mutual release, when it arrived, was as a dawning sunrise of hope in a new day. It was hope of love and hope of a future.

Intertwined in an embrace Jake hoped would never end he lifted his head stared into Jiao's eyes. "I love you Jiao."

"Of course," she answered. "I love you too."

19

Jake sat up and smiled, fortified and renewed. Jiao had taken her toiletries bag to the ladies' room and was cleaning up. Jake didn't want to be caught lounging so he slid out of the sleeping bag, scooped up his toiletries, and went into the men's room.

He took his time washing. He thought of Jiao's always neat appearance. He wanted to be as thorough. He sponged himself off, washed his hair over the sink, and shaved. He brushed his teeth and rinsed his mouth. He used his deodorant and Axe body spray. Jake grinned as he pulled up his pants. Being a fugitive on the run wasn't so bad after all.

Jake returned to the conference room and found Jiao sitting cross-legged on the floor sorting stacks of paper. He dropped his toiletries into his suitcase and came up behind her. He paused for a moment wanting to rekindle the intimacy of the previous night.

Jiao had her waist-long black hair draped over one shoulder. She turned her head toward Jake and beamed. He bent and kissed her. She cupped his face with both hands and the two shared a mouthwash scented passionate kiss. She sighed. "We should get some breakfast and tea before it gets light."

"Sounds like a plan."

They both settled for dry cereal doused in milk. They ate a half of box of Cheerios between them. Jiao brewed green tea and the two went back into their special conference room. "I don't know what I'm missing," Jiao said.

Jake looked at the organized piles of paper. "It has to be a patent. The text pointed us there."

Jiao nodded. "Maybe I was wrong about it being an energy storage patent."

"Maybe but that makes the most sense."

"There's other information that I can access. We'll have to use one of the LTE tablets."

"What other information?"

"I have some of Amrish's emails."

"Really? How?"

"When you were looking at Amrish in his office I logged on to his email." She presented Jake a sheepish expression. "I had his email password because I sent joint emails from his account from time to time."

"You don't have to explain."

"Anyway, I logged on his account, selected a page of emails he just received, and forwarded them to my Gmail account."

Jake looked at Jiao with raised eyebrows. "We need to look at those emails."

"I scanned them that morning and most looked unimportant. I went to his sent folder to delete the email I just forwarded and decided to grab a page of the most recent emails Amrish sent. I selected the page and forwarded those to my Gmail account too. Then I deleted the two emails I just forwarded to myself from the sent folder." She looked at Jake. "After seeing the philosopher's stone patent text, I didn't think about those emails. I never looked at them when I had my laptop."

"We need to see those emails. They may give us a clue to what we're missing. We should use one of those cheap tablets to access your Gmail account."

"But we don't want to give ourselves away."

Jake nodded. "We might be able to mask our use of those tablets." He went to his suitcase and extracted a plastic case. "I built a Wi-Fi sniffer from a Raspberry Pi."

"A Raspberry Pi? Isn't that a computer kit high school kids use?"

"They should use it. This little $30 computer has a quad processor and a built in Wi-Fi. I was just playing around with it and wondered if I could monitor Wi-Fi signals. It does a great job." He dug further in his suitcase and extracted a seven inch display and keyboard that fit in the palm of his hand.

Jiao laughed. "I didn't know you were a 'maker'."

"It's one of the greatest things about the Silicon Valley." He connected the display with a short HDMI video cable and used a wall plug.

"My daughter thinks technology like that is hardware without a soul." She nodded. "She's studying theater at USC."

Jake flicked the switch and was gratified to see LED lights flicker. "There is a soul in this hardware. There really is. But if your daughter looks anything like her mom, she'll be a shoe-in for a movie career."

Jiao laughed. "I'll show you a picture. My family says she does look like me."

Jake watched the loading screen boot up on the small display. He flicked the switch of the battery operated keyboard.

"Is that Bluetooth?"

"Yeah. You can't type fast on it, but it works."

"I'm glad you brought this along." She extracted a picture from her wallet and extended it to Jake. "My daughter, Michelle."

Jake turned from his screen and saw a picture of a stunning young woman. "God, she's beautiful." He laughed. "And she's a Jiao mini-me."

"Mini-me?"

"She looks like a slightly younger version of you."

"Oh, slightly younger."

"Jiao, you could pass for twenty-nine, no sweat." Jake tapped keys on the small keyboard. "Okay, let's see what we have." He frowned. "I only see five networks."

Jiao looked over his shoulder. "Those networks show their media access control MAC addresses for all to see."

"And MAC addresses identify the hardware. That's why we left our computers behind." He pointed to a portion of the display. "I'm not transmitting anything, I'm just sniffing."

"But we should only connect with a tablet. They may be able to trace the MAC address of your Raspberry Pi."

Jake nodded. "Right but I wanted to see a crowded spectrum and I only see five networks."

"It's only 6:30 a.m. Silicon Valley engineers aren't early risers. When Fry's opens I'll bet you see hundreds."

Jake flicked his Wi-Fi sniffer off. "So we wait until the airwaves get more crowded so we can get lost in the noise."

"Yes. That's our best shot at anonymity. We get lost in the noise." Jiao walked over to her stacks of papers with her hands on her hips. "I wish I'd have remembered those emails earlier but they might not tell us anything. What are we missing?"

"We've gone over and over those 221 patents. All are tweaks to existing knowledge. Most could be considered prior art."

"Most patents are evolutionary. Few things are novel."

Jake sat in his chair. "Few thing are novel . . . that would explain why someone is so paranoid."

"That's why Amrish masked his find in the noise of 221 patents. With enough noise, burying something in plain sight works." Jiao rearranged the stacks of paper. "But 221 isn't an unmanageable number. I'm missing something."

"These aren't the best of circumstances."

"I've been looking at printouts of Amrish's patents for two days."

"Are you sure you got them all?"

"Yes, I did a thorough search for any with his name. The answer's in here somewhere."

Jake went to the stacks of papers. "Where are the patents that you've given the least attention to?"

Jiao pointed to a small stack. "That pile over there is from the patent office's technology sector 1700 covering chemical and materials engineering. I've spent all my time on the patents from technology sector 2800. That's where the energy storage patents are."

"What's sector 2800?"

"Technology sector 2800 covers semiconductors, electrical and optical systems and components. All but a dozen of Amrish's patents were there."

"Makes sense." Jake picked up the small stack. "But I'll look at these chemical and material engineering patents to see if something pops up while we wait."

"I'm going to see if I missed a category in these others."

Jake waded through the chemical and materials patents. Most seemed like graduate theses on complex chemical processes and their resulting exotic compounds. He then looked at one that blended with the group but, the more he looked at it, the more it seemed out of place. The others stopped at describing chemical processes but this one described an actual device. "Jiao?"

"Yes?"

"What do you know about yttrium barium copper oxide superconductors?"

Jiao lifted her head. "They were all the rage in the 1980s."

"Why?"

"Most superconductors require near absolute zero temperature. Yttrium barium copper oxide superconductors are intriguing because they achieve zero resistance above the boiling point of nitrogen at 77° Kelvin."

"Which means what?"

"Which means we could cool the material with common liquid nitrogen. Those were called the high temperature 123 superconductors."

"123?"

"I did a graduate paper on superconductors. 123 describes the mole ratio. 1 to 2 to 3 is the mole ratio of yttrium to barium to copper. That's why it's called the 123 superconductor. What did you find?"

"I'm not sure. It seems like Amrish took a thirty year old Department of Energy chemical superconductor patent and built something with it."

Jiao laid the papers she was examining down and came alongside Jake. "Let me see."

Jake spread the papers of the patent filing out in front of them. The two huddled side by side. "See, in figure 14 here. There's a device . . ." He leaned closer to the drawing. "And right here – there's a sheath of liquid nitrogen."

"Yes, yes I see." She leaned into the drawing so close their cheeks were nearly touching.

"And this sandwich of the yttrium barium copper oxide plates is labeled a capacitor."

"Ah . . . this could be it. This is a liquid nitrogen cooled superconducting supercapacitor." As she read her smile widened. "This could be charged in seconds or trickle charged over hours. It could be cycled thousands of times. It would just need to stay cooled."

"Would it have the storage capacity to power a house?"

"It could. I'd need to look at the Department of Energy paper this patent references. It looks quite scalable."

"Why didn't anyone do anything with this technology the past thirty years?"

"I don't know. Maybe it's like the oil sands and fracking. It took the rise in price and need to make the old technology viable."

"Is this better than a fuel cell?"

"Jake, you may have found what we've been looking for."

Jake looked at his watch. "It's 10:00 a.m. I'm going to turn on my Wi-Fi sniffer." He crossed the room and booted up his homemade device. "A superconducting capacitor . . . who would have come up with that?" He tapped some keys and watched his screen. "Wow, now there are over 500 Wi-Fi sites I can see. We should be able to stay in the noise with this many."

Jiao looked up from the capacitor patent. "500 is enough noise." She looked back at the patent. "This might be it but how did Amrish use it?"

"Maybe his emails will give us a clue." Jake got up and went to the corner of the conference room. He extracted an LTE tablet. "I hope this works. I'm going to just use the Wi-Fi connection. I'll keep the cellphone radio off."

"Good idea. Whichever site you connect to will log the hardware MAC address."

"Someone can find the address of this hardware but it won't be easy for them to track it to us. We paid cash for these tablets and burner phones. Hank actually went to the counter. They never got my picture. They shouldn't be able to find us."

"Unless we make a mistake. I'd love to send an email to my daughter but that would give it away."

Jake looked at the tablet. "I should've plugged this in." He pulled out the charger and hooked it to another wall outlet. "All we do is wait, wait, wait . . . and the world is searching for us."

Jiao was still studying the patent filing. "This could be scaled quite large. It could also provide a distributed supply of direct current."

"What would that do?"

"It could provide electricity to individual houses but the real power would be in scale. This technology doesn't threaten an individual, it threatens the whole renewable energy strategy. A California state government push could make this technology deployable across the grid. It would likely get national support."

"You think the government would be trying to stop this?"

"No, California is adamant about leading in renewable energy. But I've read all the initiatives and laws . . . there's nothing on a superconductor storage device."

"So the state government doesn't know about it or they aren't interested." Jake tapped the power button of the tablet. He watched as the opening splash screen flashed on.

"The renewable energy department would be very interested."

"Then they don't know about it." Jake tapped the settings of the tablet. "Okay, we're almost up." He opened the Wi-Fi connections screen. "Let's see, here's the free Wi-Fi from Fry's. We only have one bar and it'll be crowded."

Jiao moved across the conference room and crouched beside Jake. "That's what we want. That'll keep our login record in the noise."

Jake tapped the connect button and watched the swirling timer. "Come on, you can do it." He grinned. "There." He handed the tablet to Jiao. "See if you can log onto the internet."

Jiao opened the browser. "It's slow but it's working. How much memory does this have?"

Jake looked at the LTE tablet box. "16 gigabytes with a 2 megapixel camera. Not bad for $70."

Jiao put her thumb over the camera. "The last thing we want is video to kick on. Okay, let's see if I can log on to my Gmail account. I'll try to download these messages to the memory."

"Look at that. The screen is scratched."

"Can't be helped. It's all we've got." Jiao stared at the display. "This is taking a while." She tapped in her login and password. They both watched the swirling loading indicator. The screen flashed and her emails appeared.

"There they are. It's working."

"This is going to take a while. I've got hundreds of unread emails. Let me search." Jiao pulled up the soft screen keyboard and tapped in Amrish's name. Again the two watched the loading swirl for long minutes. The screen popped up with the two forwarded emails.

The two grinned at each other. "I've got three USB thumb drives and an adapter that will connect them to this tablet. Let's save these emails to both the device and thumb drives."

Jiao opened a menu. "Here goes. I hope this has what we need."

"It has to."

20

Jake prided himself on having patience. The download of a handful of Amrish's received and sent emails tested that patience. "You've been at it for an hour."

"I'm just downloading and saving. I've downloaded those two forwarded emails to the tablet and two USB thumb drives. When this last USB drive is done, we'll disconnect from Wi-Fi and see what we have."

"I've got the second tablet charged but there's only one USB adapter."

"Just a few minutes more."

"Jiao, I'd be happy to stay with you here for weeks." He put his hand on her shoulder. His heart skipped a beat when she turned and beamed a winsome smile. "But somehow, we've got to get back to our lives." He licked his lips. "And I certainly want you in my life."

"Thank you Jake. I want you in my life too." She turned back to the screen. "There, everything's downloaded. I'll turn off Wi-Fi and we can see if these emails mean anything." She pulled the adapter and USB thumb drive from the tablet and extended it to Jake. "Before we expand on what was a wonderful night, we have to figure this out."

Jake took the USB thumb drive. "I know. Everything depends on it." He leaned in and gave her a kiss. "Now I can go to work."

The two opened the email Jiao forwarded from Amrish's account that showed received emails. Jiao managed to grab twenty-nine recently received emails from Amrish's inbox. Jake scanned the subject lines and realized most were administrative or spam; the type he would archive or delete from his own email first thing in the morning. He honed in on three emails that looked important. One was from human resources and Jake swallowed when reading that his termination package was prepared. *Amrish really was going to fire me.* Jake suppressed an unwanted surge of anger. *Focus . . . the situation is much different.*

"Did you see this one from ACES Corporation?" Jiao asked. "It was sent at 1:32 a.m. the morning Amrish was murdered."

"No, let me look."

"That's important because Amrish sent me the philosopher stone patent text at 1:34 a.m. – right after he read this one."

"Let me get it." Jake saw the email from 1:32 a.m. and opened it. "Okay, what's this about?" He read aloud. "No deal. Stop or face the consequences. Call in sick this morning so we know you accepted our generous retirement option." He looked at Jiao. "Whoa, this is why Amrish knew he was in trouble."

"That's why they killed him when he showed up for work."

"Without his laptop which probably has the superconductor patent all detailed out into new product designs."

"He never said a word of this to me."

"What's ACES Corporation?"

"I don't know. I'm going to hook back up to Wi-Fi and search for it."

"I'll check the sent messages while you do that." Jake went back to the folder on the USB drive and opened the forwarded email of sent messages. Jiao had managed to grab thirty-one sent messages. Jake first noticed a sent message to human resources about preparing his exit package. He resisted the urge to open it.

"ACES stands for Achievement of California Energy independence though Solar."

Jake turned. "Only solar?"

"It looks like it. The vision statement refers to the study about how 3,850,000 exajoules of solar energy hit the earth every year. That's more energy hitting the earth each hour than the world consumes in a year."

"That's always been the renewable energy vision. Convert enough sunlight to electricity to wean ourselves from fossil fuels."

"This is taking a while to load. ACES Corporation is an umbrella organization, incorporated in Delaware, with Asian branches based out of Hong Kong. Let's see, there's five or six U.S. operations inside that umbrella."

"All solar?"

"It looks like it. One company procures cells from China, modules from India, and assembles panels in Turlock." Jiao picked up a legal pad and pen. "I'm going to write this down. They have another company that does solar installations out of Porterville and one that offers reclamation out of Bakersfield."

"All San Joaquin Valley cities that need employment."

"They have an inverter company in Stockton and the ACES Corporation headquarters is right here in Santa Clara."

"Really?" Jake turned back to the emails and found one that Amrish sent last week with ACES in the subject line. He opened it. After reading it, he grinned. "Jiao, I found it."

She came alongside Jake, pen and paper in hand. "Show me."

"It's just what we thought. Amrish refers to ACES Corporation investment in DHS."

"I didn't know Amrish got money from ACES."

"Here he thanks someone called Arjun Azmi for the company saving investment. It looks like Amrish was trying to roll DHS under the ACES umbrella."

"Arjun Azmi is the CEO of ACES, which is the parent over all these solar companies."

"Read this. Amrish was enlisted to dig up renewable energy patents and assign them to ACES Corporation."

"That's a classic lock out technique patent trolls use. They find prior art, tweak and refile the patent to own it, and sue anyone who tries to use it. ACES was raising the barrier to entry for competitors."

"And Amrish, when filing and assigning these patents to ACES, must've accidentally stumbled on the thirty year old Department of Energy superconductor patent."

"It was dumb luck. The superconductor patents weren't even in the renewable energy category."

"According to this email, Amrish made a direct pitch to Arjun to show the energy storage prototype to Sacramento lawmakers."

"Amrish realized what he found."

"And that pitch is what Arjun refused the morning Amrish was killed?"

"Yes. There must've been phone conversations as well. Amrish alludes to a back and forth on a proposal. They went as far as to build a prototype to see if it was viable. They must've not have known what to do with the storage technology."

"Because ACES locked everything up already – at least in California – and efficient storage would turn everything on its head."

Jake lowered the tablet. "What a bastard Arjun is."

"Wait a minute," Jiao said. "Let me see that email."

Jake handed the tablet over. "What did you see?"

Jiao pointed. "Look at this. Amrish bcc'd – blind carbon copied – that email to someone named Gita Bhatt."

Jake looked over her shoulder. "And look at what Gita's email address ends with – senate.ca.gov."

"Amrish was telling someone in Sacramento, in the California state government, about it. From this note, ACES built a prototype of this storage device and it must work."

"Couldn't Arjun and the ACES Corporation secure the patent to protect the technology for themselves?"

"No way. The semiconductor equipment companies who already bloodied their noses on exotic solar cells would be all over this." Jiao shook her head. "It's materials science 101. I can't believe this superconductor storage patent was in plain sight all these years."

The realization expanded in Jake's mind. He saw these superconductor storage units at the base of every wind turbine, in every house, at every solar farm. He saw these devices storing energy from geothermal sources, wave motion, and stream water mills. All the things too small in power generation for energy on demand now made sense. "This device changes everything."

"Both Amrish and Arjun knew it."

Jake saw the net need of new generation plants from all sources decrease. He saw the sought after renewable energy dream of true worldwide energy self-sufficiency. "This storage device would solve nearly every energy and climate problem the world's facing. It is the philosopher's stone or Holy Grail." He turned to Jiao. "Why would Arjun squash it?"

"If he can postpone this technology from getting out for a few years, the ongoing installations and state contracts will expand to an unstoppable point. And with all the push on renewable energy, no one saw this patent for the last three decades." Jiao shook her head. "Other U.S. states are going after fracking, oil sands, and oil shale. If California doesn't grab this technology, it could sit undiscovered for another ten or twenty years."

"And all the problems of the world keep growing." He grimaced. "All so one greedy bastard can stay rich and powerful." He looked at Jiao. "We need to stop him."

Part III

Search

21

Jake and Jiao sat on the floor side by side against a wall in the vacant office building conference room. Jake was eating microwaved Salisbury steak dinner and Jiao was eating Yakisoba Noodles – both for the second time. "I can't believe it," Jake said. "I hoped and prayed for something like this."

"Something like what?" Jiao asked. She used her chopsticks in quick dexterous moves. "You hoped to be a fugitive on the run?"

"With the woman I love? It has its attractions."

Jiao elbowed him. "We're living in a vacant office building and likely to be discovered any moment. That's what you hoped and prayed for?"

"We're in a high stakes fight against pure evil. If we win, we change the world."

"Winning's a daunting task. I looked up Arjun the last time I logged onto Wi-Fi. Arjun Azmi and his wife Lalita are worth over a hundred million dollars, run the ACES Corporation parent company, and are well connected to Sacramento politicians."

"I don't give a damn about their wealth or position. From a character perspective they have as much value as dog shit I scrape off the bottom of my shoe."

Jiao smiled. "I agree but we're still fugitives on the run."

"Military maxims apply. The best defense is a good offense. The only way we free ourselves is to take them down." Jake rested a hand on Jiao's knee. "The only way we can be safe and together is to take them down."

"Their wealth and position make that difficult. Maybe it's better to tell the police everything."

"The police have the same emails and would have read them by now. Do you think they made the connection of Amrish to Arjun and Lalita?"

Jiao frowned. "No, they wouldn't have published our pictures in the news. We're the only ones that put this together. We're the only ones that know the technical detail of the energy storage patent. We should make evidence packs. We'll write down the detail of the patent, all the connections we found, and then link the facts. We'll wrap that paper write up around a USB thumb drive and tape it together. We can make three packs."

Jake grunted.

"What?"

"It's not enough. Hiding a patent? That makes no sense. A patent is a public disclosure."

"But even Amrish didn't put the 123 superconductor supercapacitor detail in his emails."

"He did refer to a prototype. They actually built a working storage device."

"What if we found the prototype?"

"That would be better." Jake stirred his mashed potatoes in gravy and popped a spoonful in his mouth. He swallowed and looked at Jiao. "We're on step five and the police are still on step two."

"What do you mean?"

"They wouldn't give a tinker's damn about a world changing prototype or patent. They are looking to find a cop killer."

"And they think it's us." Jiao turned to Jake. "That's what we need to find – evidence on the real killers."

Jake nodded. "We've got to pin this on the ACES Corporation and Arjun. We've got to find out how they made that exploding button."

"And who made it for them. That's how we pin these murders on them."

"Only then will the murder motive of the patent make sense."

"What are you thinking?"

"We need to go out and get more evidence."

"We can't go out in broad daylight."

"It has to be at night."

"But where?"

"Let's take a step back and map this out." Jake set his dinner tray to the side, lifted his yellow legal pad from the floor, and flipped to an empty sheet. "Let's think. One, we are facing rich, powerful, politically connected enemies both able and willing to kill to protect their position."

"It's like a television show. What's more, they did kill to protect their position."

"And framed us for it. That's why we're here eating microwaved food. We need to connect them to the killing. We need to find out about Gita Bhatt. Amrish thought she was important."

"But we don't know why. What evidence do we have?"

He exhaled. "You're right. We don't have a shred of evidence linking Arjun and ACES Corporation to the murders."

"We do have texts and emails linking them to Amrish."

"It's not enough, they did a good job framing us."

"That's number two. We need to find that connection. They couldn't have made these buttons and RF triggers on their own."

Jake wrote. "Two, we find out who produced the buttons." He nodded. "I doubt that manufacturing was outsourced."

"Good point. They probably used an old semiconductor fab right here in the Silicon Valley."

"Which involves more people."

"Then there's the question of how they got the buttons on Amrish's and Detective Delgado's shirts."

"Three, we find out how they got the buttons on their targets."

"That's more people. If you think about it, a lot of people were involved in these murders."

Jake nodded. "And a lot of people are involved in suppressing this patent – particularly since the email refers to a prototype." He shook his head. "No way did Arjun do these arrangements for the murders himself."

"I think Lalita's involved. Did you see those political pictures I downloaded? They are in everything together."

"Okay, but if they're a pair, they'd still need someone else to arrange the murders. I don't think they'd personally get their hands dirty."

"They couldn't. And they don't personally have the technical expertise to design an exploding button."

"They have people in the middle."

"Yes, but I'll bet there's just one in charge – at least for the button murders. There must be someone who they utterly trust that works all the details."

"He or she must be a shady character – able to get into cleaners, arrange secret production, and trigger the buttons at the precise time." Jake looked at his legal pad. "That's our number one action. We have to find Arjun and Lalita's trusted killer."

Jiao arose. "I'll take your garbage. We don't want this place to smell of rotting food."

Jake handed her the remains of his microwave dinner. "Thanks." He watched as she crossed the room and put the plates in a garbage bag. "You are beautiful."

Jiao turned and cocked her head. "Thank you. Will you still love me if I'm in an orange jumpsuit?"

She meant it as a joke but it chilled Jake. "Yes but Jiao we have to win this thing. It's too important."

Jiao crossed the room and crouched facing Jake. She took both of his hands in hers and fixed him in her gaze. "Powerful important people have been doing this forever. I saw this in Hong Kong and in mainland China. People with power can take everything, your money, your future, your life. It happens all the time. Don't think the U.S. is any different."

"You don't think we can win?"

"It's difficult. I saw many people, like you Jake, who believed in character. I saw many who were crushed. I don't want that to happen to you."

"Jiao, maybe we lose but we have to fight. What's the alternative?"

"We run."

"To where? Mexico? Canada?"

"Either. We go to a different country, assume different names, and start fresh. That's what my family did when we left Hong Kong. Sometimes fighting doesn't work. This is so big."

Jake looked at his legal pad. "To run means we let Arjun and Lalita get away with murder. To run means we let them bury a patent that could save the world." He looked at her. "Even if we could get away, how could we live with ourselves?"

"By living. If we lose, we lose everything, including the chance to tell the world about this patent."

"Hiding in Mexico or Canada isn't a life."

"Are you willing to spend the rest of your life in jail?"

The idea to run was tempting but flawed. "Jiao, that's just as likely to happen if we run. There's no political asylum for murderers. Mexico and Canada would extradite us. If we don't fight this now, we lose the chance to clear our name. Whatever trail that's out there on the buttons and the murders will be gone."

Jiao looked up at the ceiling. "So we fight. Win or lose, we fight."

"They have us cornered."

She tapped the legal pad. "How can we find out who Arjun has doing the killings?"

"Did you get Arjun's address?"

"Yes, he's in a mansion in Los Altos Hills."

"I'm glad Hank left us a map." Jake opened it. "I'm going on a recon mission tonight. Let's see how far Los Altos Hills is."

"If I were driving from here I'd take Foothill Expressway."

"Yeah but look, that's a lot more distance than if I just walk along El Camino Real and then take a left on Arastradero Road." His finger ran along the route. "Then a left on Fremont Road and a left on Weston Drive. I look for his mansion at the end of Weston. This is a distance of five or six miles. I'll have to keep in the shadows so it'll take me an hour and a half to get there. I'll plan on two hours to be safe."

"You're going to go to the Azmi Los Altos Hills mansion alone?"

"I don't think it's a good idea for us to go together."

Jiao pulled the map toward her. "Then I'll go to the ACES Corporation campus in Santa Clara."

"I don't want you out when I am."

"You're taking a risk to save us – so am I.

"What do you expect to find at ACES Corporation?"

"I have a hunch. I want to see if any lights are on at 2:00 a.m." She grinned. "You'd be amazed how many unauthorized things are done by lab techs in early morning hours." She tapped the map. "What do you expect to find in Los Altos Hills?"

"I don't know but their trusted mystery killer wouldn't meet them at the ACES Corporation offices. They'd more likely meet in secret at their mansion."

"Careful. There's probably as much security at their mansion as at their ACES headquarters office."

"There will be a lot of security at both places." Jake nodded. "Let's call this a dual recon mission." He picked up the empty box from one of their LTE tablets. He flipped it over and read the specifications. "These cheap tablets have a two megapixel camera. We should take pictures."

Jiao nodded. "And keep Wi-Fi off."

"Unless one of us gets caught."

Jiao inhaled. "Don't get caught."

"I'm pretty good at sneaking around."

"Both places will have infrared night vision security cameras. If they get a glimpse of our face, we'll be identified."

"How do we hide our face? Hank didn't buy us ski masks."

"I have a couple of scarves."

"You packed scarves?"

"I travel so much I have a pre-packed bag. That's what I grabbed when we left my townhouse." Jiao arose, went to her suitcase, and rummaged through a side compartment. She lifted two light scarves, one with a maroon floral pattern and the other with a blue floral pattern. "I got these at Nordstrom."

Jake crossed the room and took the blue scarf. "This will work. I'll keep it in my pocket until I get close."

"And then cover everything but your eyes. I'll do the same when I get to the ACES Corporation campus."

"If they see us, they won't be able to do a quick facial recognition scan."

Jiao nodded. "Eventually they'll figure it out."

"When too many figure it out, we're caught."

"Our freedom is sand running out of an hourglass."

"This recon could take a lot longer than we think."

"What if we can't make it back before dawn?"

"We can't walk around in daylight. If we get stuck out there past dawn, we'll have to hide until it gets dark."

"Where could we hide?"

"I ran marathons with Hank and the Processed Technologies team. We'd practice by running the levees. They go under highways and above the levee just below the highway there's a gap of about two feet where we'd often see homeless camp out in. If I'm still out at dawn, I'm going to look for an overpass or a levee bridge. That's where I'll hide."

"We're really going to do this." Jiao nodded. "I'm going to do everything I can to make it back in time. What if one of us gets back in time and the other doesn't?"

"Whoever makes it back has to wait. The other won't be able to move until it gets dark again."

"So if only one makes it back that one has to wait all day until dark for the other to be able to move."

"Right."

"Do we take our burner phones?"

Jake nodded. "Yes, but we only use the burner phone if we get caught."

"But we can't turn them on. If we do, they'll be tracked to the Los Altos mansion and the ACES Corporation campus."

Jake thought about it. "If one of us gets caught we turn on our phone and get word to Hank. If not, and only one makes it back, we wait a day."

"Like I said – let's not get caught."

22

Jake was surprised how cold it was. He walked up El Camino Real, block after block, and kept his head down. Streetlights, vehicle headlights, and light coming though glass-fronted businesses in squat buildings lit his way. He moved at a good clip to keep warm but saw cameras everywhere. *That movie The Circle has me paranoid that my every move is being captured.* He noted cameras on streetlight poles, traffic lights, and store fronts. It wasn't paranoia. There was no way to avoid his image being captured. The only thing he could do was not stand out.

He fought a rush of panic when a police car pulled to the side in front of him at the corner of El Camino and San Antonio. Jake did his level best to not alter his stride. Two policemen crossed the sidewalk in front of him, walked up San Antonio, and entered Armadillo Willy's BBQ. Jake exhaled in relief and kept moving.

Jake felt reassured, five blocks later, when he turned left onto the narrow Arastradero Road. The noble plan to fight against great evil, to defy the odds, and change the world seemed mundane as he walked alongside the Los Altos Hills road. He felt odd that this sidewalk and these trees and grass and road were all ordinary.

He was a fugitive for murder trying to clear his name. Jake was trying to right a wrong. He walked into the posh neighborhood of millionaires and no one noticed him. He approached Foothill Expressway and, before crossing it, he went to the other side of Arastradero Road and noted Bol Park Bike Path. In classic California style, there was a narrow asphalt ribbon with a yellow dashed line separating the bike lanes. He noted trees on either side.

Jake reversed course, crossed Arastradero Road again and saw a sign for Alta Mesa Cemetery and Funeral Home. He made mental note that, if he had to hide, one of these two finds could be used for escape. The bike path was good but the cemetery, creepy as it might be, was better.

He crossed Foothill Expressway, disappointed that it was a regular crosswalk with no underpass. He walked several blocks further up Arastradero Road until he saw the sign for Fremont Road. *This isn't U.S. Army land navigation, but I'm getting it done.* He walked up Fremont Road and wondered when would be the right time to put on his scarf. When he did, his face would be covered but if anyone saw him they'd think he was a burglar and sound the alarm.

He walked up Fremont Road feeling uneasy. There were too many houses and too many cameras. He walked alongside Fremont as it curved left and sucked in his breath when seeing the Weston Drive sign. *I am nuts to be doing this.* He thought of Jiao out there somewhere tracking down the Santa Clara ACES Corporation campus. He nodded to himself and walked with resolve down Weston Drive, hoping no one would see him and ask his purpose.

Jake was pleased there was no moon. He was pleased Weston Drive was dark. He did feel like a burglar in the night. He got to the end of Weston Drive and pondered the driveway angling left. *This is it.* He entered the grounds of the Azmi mansion to the left of the driveway and stopped next to a large oak tree. He surveyed the area. He could see no one and, save for the distant hum of traffic, hear no one. He pulled the Nordstrom blue floral scarf from his front pants pocket and wrapped it around his face. He knotted it feeling this unreal situation was something from a dream.

A dog barked. He hadn't thought of that. He listened and concluded that the barking dog was at least a block away. He waited and the barking ceased. He looked into the grounds. *I'm going to have to get closer to see anything.* As he looped toward the mansion, he stayed away from the driveway and extracted his tablet.

He looked at the cheap tablet and again, the feeling of unreality struck. Jiao taped paper over the LED recording light and the two tested the tablet's photographic ability before setting out. In the bright conference room the photo quality was fair. Here in the darkness, Jake wondered if he'd capture anything at all. He wondered if there was anything worth capturing and if there was, did he dare get close enough to see it?

Minutes ticked by and, although frozen in apprehension, his mind circled and circled around other ideas. Either they would turn in the information they had to the police and risk a life in jail or they try to tag the bastards framing them. Like a condemned man with a gun to his head and the proclamation 'do this or die', Jake decided to move.

He slunk in a half crouch from tree to tree deeper into the Azmi grounds. He stopped when he saw dark building outlines. Jake put his back to an oak tree. He slid his LTE tablet out of his jacket pocket. Jake turned it on and was blinded by the backlight. He pulled the tablet to his chest and swiveled away from the buildings. He waited and heard nothing. He saw a dark rectangle afterimage in the middle of his vision. *I forgot about the backlight.*

Jake paused, again debating his next move. He had to get pictures. Without pictures there was no evidence. He unzipped his coat and used it to shield the tablet's light. He pulled the tablet a couple inches away from his chest. The blinding backlight was shielded. He tapped the camera button. A live picture image appeared that looked to him as nothing but black outlines. He tapped the picture button and watched as an image was captured.

He looked up toward the buildings and waited for his eyes to adjust. Keeping the tablet's camera on and the backlight shielded, he moved closer to the buildings. He got to the crest of a small rise and saw the mansion, which was dark, and a guest house, which had lights on. There were two cars parked alongside the guesthouse. He steadied the tablet and captured an image of the buildings and cars. Jake saw from the two second image preview that he wasn't close enough to get anything more than outlines.

He slunk closer, stopped, saw a large tree right next to the guest house, and mapped a route to that tree. He lowered to a crouch and, wondering if his pounding heart would burst, crept toward the large tree in a circuitous route. Every step was an agony in hearing crackles and fearing discovery. He lowered himself to the ground as he got to the base of the tree. He looked at the tablet and noted that he took several images of the inside of his jacket.

Jake braced himself and rose on one knee. He framed a clear view of the guest house and captured the image. He swiveled toward the mansion and captured that image. He stared at the mansion and wondered why it appeared so dark. He tapped the movie icon which switched from the tablet from capturing still images to taking video. He started the video. He focused on the mansion and panned left and right.

Noises from the guesthouse caught his attention. He welded himself to the tree and swiveled that direction. The door of the guest house opened and two men exited deep in conversation. Jake pointed the tablet toward them with the video recording. He was careful to keep the backlight shielded. He heard snippets of their conversation. One man said something about 'desi mal' and later Jake heard the word 'gaandu'. He hoped the tablet's microphone was sensitive enough to capture the low conversation. The two men walked toward their parked cars and Jake saw that one wore an odd light colored blazer. The other was nothing more than a black outline. He videoed until both got into one car and drove away.

He stopped the video-recording and sunk down, heart pounding. He could still see a light coming from the guest house on the side opposite the single parked car. He calmed himself. *Did I get anything of value?* If he got anything at all it might be a piece of the conversation. But that was a big if. He rotated and looked at the guest house from the opposite side of the tree. Light was coming from the back.

Emboldened by the departure of the two, Jake snuck in the open still in a crouch alongside the building. *I'll get to the back and see if there's an unlocked door.* He knew it was a long shot but worth a try. He rounded the back of the guesthouse and saw a wood deck covered with an awning. Tables and chairs were arranged in groups on the deck. *The rich must entertain their guests after all.* Behind the deck were sliding glass doors. The shade was pulled down on one side but on the other, the shade was only two-thirds down.

Jake could see the room behind the shade wasn't well lit. He figured they kept an end table light on before they left. *No one's inside.* He crouched and looked below the shade. He saw a counter and barstools. Maybe it was only a bar but maybe something else was going on. Maybe the energy storage prototype was inside. *I need to get in there.*

He saw his tablet had timed out and turned off. He turned it back on. He took a still image of the deck and sliding doors. He realized looking at the two second image preview that it was an off center image. He eased the tablet from his jacket and steadied it for a better picture.

Two flood lights snapped on, blinding him. He gasped and froze for an instant. He'd been seen. He turned and ran opposite the lights. Jake ran a short distance and hid behind the first large tree he saw. He leaned against the tree. *Stupid. Stupid. A camera got me.* He panted, pulled out the tablet, and turned it off. He put the tablet in his jacket pocket and zipped it closed. He shuddered. Now chilled, he zipped up his jacket. He debated making another approach at the guest house. *No, that's done. I got something. I need to head back to our hideout before dawn.*

He looked to orient himself as his night vision recovered from the floodlights. A humming sound caught his attention. He turned to the guest house. An airborne drone's light flashed on. *Damn!* Jake turned away from the drone and ran. He heard the drone's propeller whine change and realized it was following him.

Jake ran away from the grounds and found himself in a large open area. He ran at an angle opposite the grounds across an open field. The drone whine increased in pitch and menace. He visualized the drone following and capturing his desperate gait as he crossed the open area.

The security chief watched, with a perplexed expression, as the red infrared image ran across Esther Clark Park. There were few pranksters in Los Altos Hills and, the few there were, would go after the mansion. The neighborhood had Halloween instances of toilet paper in trees or eggs thrown on houses or even a smashed pumpkin. Those were the harmless security events.

But someone with a camera snuck up to the back of their guest house. That was a threat. He watched as the infrared image of a running man crossed the center of the park. *Laksh would agree, this is a threat.* The security chief made his decision. He flipped the drone toggle switch to 'arm'.

Jake ran at the pace of a quick jog. The drone sound hadn't changed. It maintained its distance as he jogged. He wondered when the drone would give up the chase.

"Trespasser," a speaker from the drone blared at Jake. "Stop immediately or face use of deadly force."

Deadly force? An armed drone in Los Altos Hills? That seemed a hollow threat but Jake flat out sprint toward a copse of trees at the end of the park. He juked around a tree and heard a dull thudding impact of something hitting the tree. *They just shot at me!*

Jake ran like a madman, powered by an adrenalin surge. He ran past houses and zig-zagged around trees. He had only one directional thought – cross Foothill Expressway and get to the cemetery. There were enough headstones and structures there to fend off this attack. He stumbled on a road and noted it was Manuela Avenue. The name meant nothing but the direction was right.

He ran alongside Manuela Avenue with his marathoner's stamina, hearing the drone maneuver behind him. Jake ran like a running back that was dodging tacklers by changing direction every few steps. He knew from his hunting experiences that nothing was easier to hit than a target moving in a straight line. As Manuela Avenue curved left he saw a wide road to the right. *Foothill Expressway! That's what I've got to cross.*

Jake stumbled down an embankment and, seeing a gap between fast moving cars, ran across the expressway. Just as he got to the other side something slammed into his back, just below the shoulder blade. He let out a wail and fell. He clawed himself up, his right arm numb, and pain shooting through his shoulder. He stumbled across a small road and into the cemetery. He dropped to his hands and knees and crawled around tombstones.

The drone's whine followed him across the expressway but, as he got deeper into the cemetery, the whining sound lessened. He fought against pain and continued snaking around the headstones. When the drone sound was well and truly gone Jake stopped. He was drenched in sweat and trembling from shock.

Pain shot through his right side. He wiped the sweat with the back of this left hand and looked at the headstone in front of him. He dumbly read the name, "Steven Paul Jobs, 1955 – 2011. I thought he was in an unmarked grave." There was something ironic about being hunted down by an authoritarian force at the burial place of someone committed to individuality.

Jake reached under his limp right arm and felt for the wound. He wailed when the slightest contact resulted in a shot of pain. *I'm hurt. What do I do now?*

23

Jiao moved in a quick gait block by block from their Sunnyvale hiding place and saw from a sidewalk sign she was in Santa Clara. This area, much more than Hong Kong, was home. Santa Clara, the heart of Silicon Valley, was where she grew up. When her young husband died of cancer and her daughter was ensconced in boarding school, there was nothing left but her work.

She loved the focus and endless challenge. Solving technology problems in a lab became her forte. No one could match her focus and stamina of sheer hours worked once she got a hold of a tough problem. Jiao stopped at an intersection waiting for the crosswalk pedestrian light with two other people. She stood behind them to avoid being noticed. The pedestrian light changed. Jiao walked behind them until across the road. She went left when the other two went straight. She pulled the collar of her jacket forward and tucked her long hair inside.

Jiao thrived in solving tough technology problems but solving a challenge of good versus evil was a new experience. The stakes were high. She was accused of murder due to a love triangle between her, Amrish, and Jake. It was ridiculous. But it was true. She had loved Amrish. At least she thought she did. She certainly loved his tenacity when DHS was struggling. And she loved Jake.

Jake was something different. He was like one of those 'do good at all costs' cowboys from old westerns. He even looked like the movie icon Alan Ladd in the movie *Shane*. She chuckled and then a somber thought struck her. *Shane survived in the end. Jake is like one of those idealistic patriotic movie heroes that sacrifice all and gets killed in the end.* She loved Jake and she feared for him. The headlights of an approaching car reminded her to save some concern for herself. Jiao lowered her head as the car passed.

She wanted to call her daughter. In the not too recent past, all she would need is a quarter and a payphone. But payphones were gone and quarters bought nothing more than a gumball these days. No, she'd have to sort this out first and tell her daughter of the adventure afterwards.

In the jumble of emotions, fear, and action; Jiao felt alive. She couldn't describe it and though it could end in an instant, the in-the-moment tension gave her a rush she'd never felt before. Maybe they win and maybe they lose but Jake and Jiao weren't hiding in a corner waiting for someone to save them. She walked the final blocks toward her destination firm in purpose.

Jiao was pleased to be so close to the ACES Corporation campus. There was something familiar about the area but the shiny new ACES Corporation headquarters campus was like many other areas of the Silicon Valley, repurposed beyond recognition of its past use. She walked on the sidewalk past the campus, went a block away, made a right, walked a block, and made another right. She approached the campus from a different direction.

What she saw was impressive. There was a green LED lit ACES corporate logo that occupied a quarter of the six story dark glass building she faced. The green color symbolized its renewable energy pitch – Achievement of California Energy independence though Solar. Jiao was committed to renewable energy herself. It grated her that a deceptive company prevented the release of the most disruptive electrical storage technology since the invention of the lead acid battery.

Silicon Valley entrepreneurs, like Steve Jobs, were supposed to be the good guys that enabled the impossible with insanely great ideas. This ACES corporate farce was something different. Jake was right, this was a fight against evil, no matter how ill advised the struggle. Jiao stood in the shadow half a block away and stared at the garish logo. She considered her next move. Jake probably had an easy time scouting a residence. Jiao knew that the ACES Corporation security would be formidable.

The ACES Corporation campus wasn't fenced but was surrounded by highly landscaped four foot high berms. Between the berms and the buildings were rows of parking spaces – wide open space. Jiao knew the wide open parking spaces covered with asphalt were, without question, monitored by night-vision cameras. *How do I get close enough to see anything?* She decided to keep her distance. She doubled back, made a right, walked a block, made another right and approached the campus for a third time.

The buildings on the backside of the ACES campus had a more reserved logo. She walked to the edge of the end building and saw white signs. She scanned the buildings and noted two loading docks. One of the loading docks had a DHL labeled trailer backed into it. She could see the sliding door behind the truck was closed.

She extracted her tablet, turned it on and jolted when the backlight lit. She pulled it to her chest, turned on the camera, and as carefully as she could, took a picture of the loading dock. *Maybe that's all I get.* She looked across the street from the campus and noted lights coming through the window of another building.

Jiao stared at those lights a long moment. Something was very familiar about that building. She turned her tablet off and, staying a half block away from the ACES campus, crossed the street. She had to see why that building was so familiar. She walked a block parallel to the building and then went to the corner. She remembered. *This is an old fab.* She tried to recall the last time she was inside.

Fifteen – no – twenty years earlier, she went to this semiconductor fabrication facility and helped install what was then a state of the art processing tool for six-inch silicon wafers. This was one of those small Silicon Valley companies that strove to offer customized silicon chips as a counter to the massive investment required to compete at scale with the large companies. The early 1980s building architecture was what looked so familiar.

But that fab, like most other small semiconductor fabs, failed to make enough profit competing with the bigger companies. Jiao remembered there was talk of auctioning the equipment from this facility. Most small fabs were either razed or shuttered and vacant. This one wasn't. Jiao moved to the front for a closer look.

The building was one story. From ground to roof were panels of crushed rock separated by long vertical rectangles of mirrored glass. The building had a flat roof bordered with curved tile awnings and topped with several tons of equipment used for heating, ventilation, and air conditioning – and a large device that provided chemical abatement and scrubbing of semiconductor process gases. Jiao stared at the roof and noted the familiar plume of steam rising from the equipment. *This fab is still being used.* That was worth capturing.

Jiao turned on her tablet, shielded the light, and took several pictures of the odd building. An old semiconductor manufacturing facility may not be able to produce competitive silicon chips but it darn sure could produce an exploding button. She noted a single car parked beside the door. The car was under a dim streetlight and, like so many in parking lots at the wee hours of the morning, would go unnoticed. She felt this find was more significant than the ACES building and resolved to get an image of the license plate.

She went up to the street paralleling the building and then cut in from the sidewalk to a copse of trees directly opposite the car. She extracted her scarf, wrapped her face, and moved forward. She leaned against one of the trees and used her tablet to capture images of the car and building. She kept the backlit screen fully hidden and took dozens of images from different angles to ensure she had the best chance of capturing the license plate.

Two bright headlights of a vehicle entering the parking lot arrested Jiao's attention. She caught her breath as the vehicle which just entered the parking lot pulled alongside the car she was photographing. She captured more images as two men got out of the car. She noted one had on a slim fitted pink blazer and the other appeared dressed in black. She kept capturing images as the two, deep in a conversation she couldn't make out, entered the building.

Jiao took two more steady images of the cars and two more of the building's roof showing the plume of steam. Jiao knew she was onto something. She toggled her tablet off and secured it in an inside pocket. She stepped straight back until she got to the sidewalk, unwrapped the scarf from her face, and began walking back toward their hiding place.

When she was six blocks from the ACES campus an awful thought occurred to her. No one would conclude mischief from the images she took. They were significant to her and Jake because they connected the dots from Amrish's emails. Would Detective Abbott or this mystery Gita Bhatt woman give them more than a passing glance?

She considered going back. Perhaps she was too cautious in getting information. She looked at her watch and realized she was nearly out of time. If she was going to get back to their hiding place before dawn she had to keep moving. She hoped Jake would be there waiting for her.

Jiao was relieved to cross Lawrence Expressway and walk past the Shell station. She walked a block into the shadows, made a left, walked another block, and crossed the parking lot to their vacant building hideout. She opened the door and closed it behind her. "Honey, I'm home." She thought Jake would appreciate the clever greeting but she heard nothing in response.

She went to their conference room, checked the food stocked break room, and called into both restrooms. No Jake. She looked out the window at the brightening sky and felt her stomach knot. *Jake, love, what have you gotten yourself into?*

24

Jake wondered if he were delirious. The pain was playing tricks on his mind. The constant pain so overwhelmed his ability to think he wondered if he had made a terrible mistake. He lifted his good shoulder off of the damp earth and got his bearing. *That's right. I'm under the Homestead Road overpass that crosses Interstate 85.*

He mentally retraced his steps from the Alta Mesa Memorial Park cemetery. Jake concluded while puzzling about the Steve Jobs headstone that the reason the drone retreated was that the armed drone only had two shots. One hit the tree when he was running across the park and the other caught him in the back below the shoulder blade. The pain in that area now consumed him.

While in the cemetery agonizing about his pain he had heard the distant hum of another drone. The hum turned into a whine and Jake knew with a certainty he would've bet his life on the sound came from a rearmed drone coming back to finish the job. The fear of instant death spurred him onward.

He ran through the cemetery until he got to El Camino Real. He still heard the dull hum of the drone, concluded it was searching the cemetery for his unburied body, and ran down El Camino for several blocks. He came to San Antonio Road and, thinking to fully confuse his pursuer, turned right. He used his stamina to run for a mile and a half and didn't stop until he got to Foothill Expressway.

Seeing the Foothill Expressway sign startled him. He wasn't thinking clearly and had looped to less than a mile from the Azmi mansion – where the attack began. He turned left and jogged alongside Foothill Expressway toward South Los Altos and Sunnyvale. He tried to get his bearings but the pain and shock made him loopy.

After nearly an hour of start stop jogging he saw a sign for Homestead Road. He realized where he was and he looked at his watch. He wasn't going to make it back to their hiding place before dawn. He saw the Homestead Road and Interstate 85 overpass and decided on his daylight hiding place.

He went under Homestead Road, thankful for the darkness. There was a large embankment underneath Homestead that led down to Interstate 85. He marveled at the amount of space. He went to a tree that was close to the underside of Homestead. He heard a groan and smelled urine. He nodded. *If a homeless person is here, this is the right place.* He leaned against a tree, winced at the pain, and closed his eyes.

Jake covered his escape in his mind. Perhaps he didn't make a mistake. He'd be tough to track. If a camera on Foothill Expressway caught his flight, wounded and all, there was nothing he could do about it. The task was to live and to hide until dark. Once it was night, he would make his way back to Jiao.

Jiao! Oh sweet God in heaven above, spare her the pain I'm going through. The constant throbbing pain as he lay on the damp earth under the overpass slowed his thoughts. Cars and trucks zoomed above him on Homestead and below him on Interstate 85 in an increasing steady stream. The smell of exhaust at first irritated him, then he didn't notice it.

Jake drooled, panted, and dozed. He opened his eyes after what felt like minutes and felt a pinch in his neck. He swung his left hand to his neck and wailed when the movement caused a bolt of pain. He found an ant on his neck and killed it by rolling it around in his fingers. He noticed it was daylight.

The interstate was bustling traffic. Jake looked at the shadows and thought it must be close to noon. It was warm and dank. He wondered if he'd be able to move when the time came. He wondered how bad his injury was. But there was nothing he could do in the daylight. He closed his eyes and dozed again.

He opened his eyes and saw it was dark. *How did that happen so fast?* The traffic below was uneven. Time was moving in fits and starts. Jake lifted his head and felt intense dryness in the back of his throat. When he blinked it felt as if his eyelids rubbed his eyes with sandpaper. It was dark, he had no idea what time it was. He had to move. Jake lifted himself and groaned.

"Hey man, are you alive up there?"

Jake focused on the sound. He saw someone through the haze of his vision climb up the sloped embankment toward him. "Wait . . ."

"Man you are fucked up." A filthy bearded man was staring at him. "You need to forage during the day and sleep at night. You got it ass backwards."

Jake did his level best to rise. He swung his legs to point toward Interstate 85 and slid a foot down the embankment. He lifted his torso and groaned. The man came beside him. The man stank but Jake's pain and his need overcame the smell. "Water?"

"You fucked that up too. Never, never, be without water." The man stared at him a long moment. "Shit, I just scored a case. I'll spare you a bottle if you promise me one thing."

"What?" It took extreme effort to give that one word answer.

The man ignored the question. He scrambled halfway down the embankment to a mounded stash beside a cluster of bushes. He returned with a bottle of water. "You don't belong here. One look and we see that." He extended the bottle. "When you get out of here, return the favor. You got to help us."

Jake took the bottle and pinned it between his knees. He unscrewed the cap with his left hand, grasped the bottle, and lifted it to his lips. The water was tepid but its wetness tasted like nectar of the gods. He drank half the bottle and was amazed at the rejuvenating effect. He looked at the bedraggled man in front of him. "Thank you. I'm not sure what, but I'll do something for you."

"Get out of my house."

Jake moved out of the underpass and went tree to tree up the embankment until he was on a road parallel to the interstate. He nodded to himself. *I know where I am. My brain may have been addled yesterday but at least I hid next to a prime route back to Sunnyvale.* His right arm was numb but the water and the walking warmed the muscles of his legs. He looked at his watch. It was 1:35 a.m.

He suppressed the desire to drink the last of the water his Good Samaritan provided. Jake knew he could push his stamina for one big physical effort. It was like the last six miles of a marathon. No matter how tired, he could still move. He would use that last effort to get to Jiao.

He prayed she avoided danger and was waiting for him. Jake walked along the road parallel to Interstate 85 until he saw it merge onto the highway. He veered left and, seeing the steady flow of cars, realized being alongside the interstate was a good way to get caught.

He moved further left between buildings and found himself on Belleville Way. This was not on his handmade map but he knew from the Interstate 85 traffic he was going the right direction. He followed Belleville for a mile until he got to Fremont Avenue. He grinned through the haze of his pain. *I know where Fremont goes.* He made a right on Freemont and covered another mile in twenty minutes. There at 2:40 a.m. facing Sunnyvale-Saratoga road, he drank the last of his water and gave thanks to whatever deity was helping him.

Jake walked for another twenty minutes and grinned when Sunnyvale-Saratoga turned into South Mathilda Avenue. His gait wasn't fast but it was steady. The numbing pain in his shoulder increased but, in his mind's eye, he saw a bright light in front of him that represented relief. He was walking toward Jiao. He made a right onto Evelyn Avenue and walked to Wolf Road. He made a left. *This gets me to Arques. From there, I'm home free.*

He was startled to see it was 4:05 a.m. by time he got to Arques. *What happened to the time?* He made a right and walked alongside Arques, past Fry's Electronics, and then veered right into the parking lot of the ugly white and blue glass building. Nothing had ever looked so welcome. He went to the door and shook it. It was locked. He shook it again.

The door popped open. Jiao grabbed his jacket at chest level and yanked him into their hiding place. She latched the door behind him. "Where were you?"

"Guest house . . . drone . . ." Now that Jake had reached his promised land his focus flagged. "Must sit." Jake sank and Jiao's arms encircled him. "Ow!"

Jiao pulled her hand back and stared at blood with wide eyes. "You're hurt."

Jake unzipped his jacket pocket and handed the tablet to Jiao. He felt like a spy delivering the critical piece of information. "Pictures . . . video."

"You're really hurt." Jiao took the tablet and draped one of Jake's arms over her shoulder. She got Jake moving and didn't stop until she got him into the men's room. She turned on the bright florescent lights and looked at the bloody patch on his jacket. "Was that from a gunshot?"

"Drone."

"Drone? I've got to see the wound and get you cleaned up." She put the tablet on the sink, and started to peel Jake's jacket off.

"Ow, ow!"

She gingerly got Jake's jacket and shirt off over his groans of pain. She leaned him over the sink. "Stay here, I've got to get my first aid and sewing kit."

"And water. I need more water."

"I'll bring some." Jiao took the tablet and disappeared.

Jake felt a jolt of pain with every heartbeat but still felt he had achieved something of great importance. No matter what might happen, he got back to Jiao. And, no matter if his tablet got nothing legible in its pictures or video, one thing was certain – he'd poked the hornet's nest.

Jiao returned and was all business. She put two cups on the sink. Jake reached for one. "Water."

"Not that one," Jiao said. "I heated that water in the microwave to clean your wound." She pushed the other cup toward him. "This is for you to drink."

Jake drank the water and sighed. "I need to eat."

"We'll have a feast but first I have to take care of this mess."

"Mess?"

"Stay still. You got hit with something like those barbed balls." She put on her reading glasses and poised over his wound with a small set of tweezers. "I can see a lot of specks. I need to get them out. With all your military training you still got chased by a drone?"

"There's something going on there. At the Azmi compound they are hiding . . . ow, that hurts."

"Stay still. I got the first one and there are dozens."

Jake did his best to not jerk as Jiao's dexterous movements removed the tiny pieces of metal. He knew he was in good hands but the unremitting pain was almost too much. He wanted to tell Jiao about his courage during his perilous adventure but he could no more than grunt between gritted teeth. Each time Jiao's tweezers moved Jake felt a sharp pin prick of pain. He drank more water and braced to endure. The pin pricks of pain slowed and then stopped.

"There, now I'm going to wash it."

"Good." Jake felt a warm washcloth placed on his wound. "Ow."

"You're lucky they hit you there. Your jacket stopped a lot of the damage. If we can stop infection, you should be fine."

"Thanks Jiao. I can't tell you how relieved I was to get back."

"I can't tell you how angry I was when you didn't make it back. I had a hellish day worrying about you. I'd almost given up hope by the time you showed up."

"I need to eat."

"No, you need to wash. You are filthy."

"I spent the day under an overpass. A homeless guy helped me."

"I hope you packed a clean change of clothes. What you're wearing is ruined. You wash. I'll bring in your suitcase. Don't put on a shirt. I'll rig some type of bandage."

"Yes ma'am. We're you in the military or something?"

"My family was stricter than your military."

"I don't know about that."

Jiao disappeared for a moment. She returned rolling his suitcase into the men's room. "I'll pull out your food. You wash."

Jiao left and Jake felt gratitude for her concern as he stared at his disheveled mirror reflection. He stripped naked and washed. He was amazed at the quantity of crusted blood and dirt he scrubbed off. He dried himself off as best he could with his towel and concluded that the sages were right – cleanliness was next to godliness. He pulled on his boxer-briefs and his pants. "Okay Jiao." He opened the men's room door and went across the hall into the conference room.

Jiao started and turned to him. Her eyes were shining. "Jake, I looked at your pictures and video. I wish I'd have thought to take video."

"Did we get anything?"

She crossed the room and clasped the shoulder on his uninjured side. "Yes we did. Between the two of us, we got a lot. I need to wash your wound again. I have a dry cloth to use as a bandage and a luggage strap should hold it in place."

"Then we need to eat."

Jiao laughed. "We have a lot of food left. We'll have a feast."

"I like your laugh."

"I was so worried about you."

"After we eat let's look at our information so we can hit those bastards a lot harder than they hit me."

25

Arjun stood next to Laksh and Lalita, staring at the pictures in disbelief. "They came after us? We've got a statewide manhunt going on for two cop killers and, in the middle of the night, they crawl out from whatever rock they're hiding under and come after us?"

Lalita slid both pictures in front of her. One picture was of a man, almost certainly Jake Hawes, face wrapped with a scarf with a tablet in front of him, squinting in the glare of floodlights from the guesthouse of the Azmi Los Altos Hills mansion. The other picture was taken miles away from their mansion. It was an image from an infrared illuminated night vision camera mounted at the loading dock of the ACES Corporation campus. A woman, who looked a lot like Doctor Jiao Liu, was facing the dock. She also appeared to have a recording device of some type.

"No one could have anticipated this boldness," Laksh said. "Besides, Jake may be dead."

"Don't you think we'd have heard about it if a dead man was found in the cemetery?" Lalita asked.

"He got out of the cemetery," Laksh replied. "We searched every stone by drone that night. He could be dead under a tree somewhere. Homeless are found dead curled up under trees all the time."

"Or one of your victims like Tommy is found dead under a tree after you're done with him." Arjun wasn't happy.

"Tommy got what was coming to him," Laksh replied.

"We're not talking about Tommy." Lalita's voice dripped cool fury. "We must destroy Jake Hawes and Jiao Liu." She stared at the pictures. "And whomever is helping these pitiful piss ants."

"What makes you think someone is helping them?" Laksh didn't like the situation. "We know Jake is a combat veteran. Maybe this was a misguided sense of heroics."

"He came to our house!"

"I think Lalita is right," Arjun said. "They're getting help." He shook his head. "But I don't think it's from Hank Rudzinski. We've been checking his smartphone signal. He's been at work and was at Lake Tahoe last weekend."

"He was also a combat veteran. Maybe they're trying to throw us off." Laksh said.

"That's not the direction the police are going. My contact has me more concerned about a threat from Sacramento."

Lalita's eyes bore into Arjun. Nearly overcome by fury, she spit out her words. "What are you saying?"

"Amrish was going crazy. He sent me an email that he wanted to show the energy storage prototype to Sacramento lawmakers."

"I remember," Lalita said. "That's why Amrish's family is in mourning."

"The Santa Clara Crime lab's REACT – rapid enforcement allied computer team – task force where able to discover that Amrish blind copied that same descriptive email to a state senator named Gita Bhatt."

"Amrish?" Lalita said the name between clenched teeth. "I told you Arjun. I told you that Amrish never understood the rules. He was to stay in his place. He aspired to a much higher rank."

"Didn't you tell me, sweet Didi, that aspiration is a disease here?" Laksh smiled. "No matter. We are still about to secure a permanent place for our family, future, and fortune."

"Laksh what have you learned since you were a boy and got to carry a rifle for the first time?"

"I learned much since then Didi. I know how to kill."

"Then you know to never leave a wounded tiger in the jungle. This Jake will come back for us."

"Jake Hawes is not a tiger, nor is Jiao Liu."

"You siblings are a sight to behold," Arjun said, "but this situation is expanding in an unacceptable manner. Every time we exert force to quash our opposition we find more opposition. We are unaccustomed to boldness in our enemies. Jake had the temerity to come to our home, Jiao had the temerity to come to our business, and Amrish had the rebelliousness to involve a state senator. We must better coordinate our actions to achieve our purpose."

"You never wanted involved in the details," Lalita said. "You wanted to stay above it all."

Arjun gave his wife the sternest look custom and presence would allow. "Dear, killing Detective Delgado may have been a satisfying show of force but it puzzled Detective Abbott. He doesn't see how Jake could've killed Delgado. In addition to searching for Jake Hawes and Jiao Liu, he's now looking elsewhere. And in doing that, he discovered Amrish's email to California State Senator Gita Bhatt."

"I thought Senator Gita Bhatt was bought and paid for," Laksh said.

Arjun sighed. "That's not how it works here. We gave her campaign a sizable donation and because of that we have access and influence. But Senator Bhatt, much like the others in Sacramento, really believe in renewable energy." He smiled. "As do we – as long as it serves our purpose."

"Our fortune and power come from more than renewable energy," Laksh said. "We get more value from shipping solar modules here than from the state contracts." He reached in his pocket and set four pill packages in front of Arjun as if they were playing cards. "The solar cells go to Mumbai from China. We then assemble the cells into modules with this valuable material sandwiched inside. Then we ship it to Turlock and assemble the modules into panels." He grinned. "After we remove this valuable packing." He pointed to the pill cards. "Our west coast distribution network is expanding. There's a big market for desi mal . . . high grade heroin that increases our power and wealth."

"Our motto of family, future, and fortune rests on power," Arjun said. "Our soon to be signed fifty-year contracts will secure our family influence and fortune in California and the United States long into the future."

Lalita pointed to the pill packs. "This will help secure our future as well."

Arjun pointed to the pills in front of him. "These are literal opiates for the masses that will help keep everyone else in their rank."

"And thwart these petty aspirations," Lalita said. "Desi mal helps our family in India, fills our accounts with money, and destroys the weak. Between the state energy contracts and desi mal, we'll secure our position and our fortune for all time."

"We must take the long view," Arjun said. "We must be in positon the next election cycle to place our family in government positions. My daughter and my nephew are poised to win elections next year. We'll start at the state level and then win at the national level. Our charitable reputation must be above reproach. These things we do now must remain in the shadows."

"Agreed but we must press on," Lalita said. "The energy storage patent is too threatening. This is not the time for squeamishness."

"No one is squeamish," Arjun replied. "But our actions have increased our enemies. As we said, they are bold enemies and one is wounded. They are desperate. They may resort to desperate moves much like Amrish."

"We must kill them all," Lalita said. "Our problems are not due to our action but due to our hesitation. We should have killed Amrish a month ago and this would have stopped there."

Laksh's interest was piqued. "Kill more than Jake and Jiao?"

"Yes," Lalita replied. "This is not about containment. This is about power – raw, unchallenged, unquestionable power." She tapped the offending pictures. "We must ensure no one dares lift a finger against us again."

"Lalita dear, surely you're not suggesting we assassinate a state senator."

"We do what we must. We do it in a way that no one will ever challenge us again."

"Then it's good Jake and Jiao haven't been caught," Laksh said.

"Why?"

"We can keep the frame going. If we have to kill the good senator, it should be Jake that gets the blame. If we have to kill Detective Abbott and members of the computer task force, Jake and Jiao get the blame."

"I have no objection to applying whatever force necessary," Arjun said. "But we must not underestimate our enemy again. When we strike, it must be decisive."

Lalita came alongside her husband and took his arm. "We are so close to achieving our design. We must not falter now."

"We won't."

26

Detective Abbott looked at his black armband and suppressed a surge of anger. He needed to be calm but a thorn of dread tempered his anger. Something didn't ring true. Detective Delgado's murder wasn't as cut and dried as the news made out. And that scared Abbott. If they were wrong, and Jake didn't murder Delgado, that meant someone else knew about that breakfast meeting. That meant someone inside the police department betrayed a fellow officer.

Abbott lifted a cup of coffee and drank the strong brew. He stared at his computer screen. The REACT task force uncovered several disturbing facts. The first was that Doctor Jiao Liu, the moment Abbott and his team started investigating Amrish Cheena's murder, extracted and saved some of Amrish's emails. That wasn't a cover up. She was looking for answers.

The second disturbing fact was that Amrish had sent a highly connected and powerful executive, Arjun Azmi, an email requesting they show an energy storage prototype to Sacramento lawmakers. The timing of the responses to this email were significant.

Arjun replied to Amrish at 1:32 a.m. telling him 'No deal. Stop or face the consequences. Call in sick this morning so we know you accepted our generous retirement option.' It was a direct threat. Moments later, at 1:34 a.m. Amrish sends a philosopher's stone patent message to Jiao and says he's in danger. The following morning Amrish is killed.

But Amrish did something else. He blind copied California State Senator Gita Bhatt on his energy prototype storage email to Arjun. There was something to that. It bothered Detective Abbott that Arjun just happened to be head of the well-regarded ACES Corporation. Even the name ACES stood for a carefully constructed marketing pitch – Achievement of California Energy independence though Solar. This whole thing stunk to high heaven long before Detective Delgado met Jake Hawes for breakfast.

If that weren't enough, there were the flagged images captured two nights ago. An image of a woman fitting Jiao Liu's description was captured walking corporate campuses near the ACES Corporation headquarters at midnight. An image of a man fitting Jake's description was captured walking on Foothill Expressway, near Arjun Azmi's mansion at 3:44 a.m. That was thirty-four minutes after a report of an unlicensed drone flying in the upscale Los Altos Hills neighborhood.

These were odd actions for a couple of murderers on the run. They were the actions of people gathering information. *But what? What does ACES Corporation and the Azmi's have to do with any of this?* He considered the possibility that Jake Hawes and Jiao Liu didn't kill Amrish. If they didn't, they would be trying to find out who did.

But Delgado's murder was the hardest to figure. His partner was going to arrest Jake at breakfast but wanted to give him one last chance to turn on Doctor Jiao Liu. Jake had to know arrest was likely but he came anyway. Detective Delgado, per procedure, had recorded every moment of the breakfast up to and including his own death.

Abbott had listened to his partner's recording of that breakfast over and again. Jake didn't add any detail about why Doctor Liu would murder Amrish. Instead, he babbled on about a patent and peak to trough energy use and how storage was the Holy Grail of renewable energy. They confirmed when they got a hold of Jake's phone the blatant threat in the text message from a burner phone: 'Jake – stop looking for answer to Amrish's death or Jiao and Hank will die. We will save you from jail and provide proof of our reach.'

Detective Delgado laughed when Jake showed him that message at breakfast. Detective Abbott, just back from Delgado's funeral, wasn't laughing. He was seething. He knew the Hank on the text was Hank Rudzinski, a personal friend of both Jake Hawes and Doctor Jiao Liu. They were actively monitoring Hank's smartphone locations and contacts and saw no recent contact with the fugitives.

Detective Abbott's request to discuss the case with Arjun Azmi was pointedly refused. Azmi was too well connected and shielded by layers of lawyers. *A powerful connected executive acts above my reach? Not on my watch. I will find a way.* In a grating ironic twist, his request to talk to California State Senator Gita Bhatt was approved.

"Detective Abbott, please pick up line two," the intercom blared.

Abbott saw the flashing light. He put on his phone headset and punched the flashing button. "Hello, this is Detective Abbott."

"Detective sir, this is the assistant to Senator Bhatt. We'll connect you now."

Abbott wondered what it'd be like to be feted hand and foot like the state senator. He waited as seconds ticked by and then a crisp voice came through his headset. "Detective Abbott, this is Senator Bhatt, how may I help you?"

"Yes senator, thank you for your time. I'll be as brief as possible. I'd like to ask you a few questions regarding a case we're working."

"Of course, go ahead."

"How do you know Amrish Cheena?"

"I don't know Amrish Cheena."

"But you received an email from him four days ago."

"Detective, all government officials have to guard against information overload. My emails are filtered by my staff."

"You never saw an email from Amrish Cheena?"

"That's correct."

"Amrish thought this was very important. He copied you on this email just before he was murdered."

"Detective, I don't know how I can help you with that."

"The email was about a patent for an energy storage device. Amrish called it the philosopher's stone patent."

"Energy storage?"

"Yes, Amrish sent the email to Arjun Azmi of ACES Corporation and requested that they show Sacramento lawmakers the prototype of an energy storage device. Does that mean anything to you?"

There was a long pause on the line. "ACES Corporation and energy storage? And murders are connected with this?" Another long pause. "This is of grave concern."

"What does ACES Corporation have to do with Sacramento?"

"They're poised to become California's largest renewable energy contractor."

"And storage devices are part of that contract?"

"No, there are no non-automotive storage devices in any state contract. We would be most interested in a working device."

"How big – how many dollars – would the ACES Corporation renewable energy contract be?"

"Detective, this is a sensitive state government negotiation."

"Look, I'm not trying to throw a monkey wrench into the state's renewable energy plans. I've got reason to believe someone in ACES Corporation wants that storage device suppressed. I want to know if the contract is big enough to be a motive for murder."

"Detective Abbott, as I said, this is sensitive information but it will be made public in the next five or six weeks. Please keep this information out of the news until then."

"I will."

"I have your personal assurance?"

"You do."

"The renewable energy negotiations with ACES Corporation are for a fifty year contract worth seventy-eight billion dollars."

"Did you say seventy-eight billion dollars?"

"Yes, over a fifty year span."

Abbott whistled. This was bigger than he imagined. These were bigger and longer timeframe financial stakes than he'd ever heard of. "Senator, what would a storage device that has something to do with peak to trough energy use do to this contract?"

Again a long pause. "The only energy storage legislation we sponsor is for emergency use of batteries in electric vehicles. A storage device of sufficient scale to store energy in trough time periods for use in peak time periods could change everything."

That's exactly what Jake was telling Detective Delgado. "This storage device would make the ACES Corporation contract worth much less?"

"It would prompt a renegotiation of those contracts. The ACES Corporation contracts would be worth less – maybe nothing at all – if the storage device could be built at the right quantity and scale. Detective, do you believe such a storage device design exists?"

"Senator, someone built a working prototype."

"We would like to see that prototype."

"So would we."

"Senator, one last thing."

"Of course."

"Please write down three names for your staff to look out for. If any of these three people contact you, please let me know right away."

"Okay."

"Please be alert for email or phone contact from Jake Hawes, Doctor Jiao Liu, and Hank Rudzinski."

There was a pause on the line. "Detective, what would you like me to do if one of these people contact me?"

Abbott thought about that. He smiled. "Tell them you believe them and set up a meeting. Of course, let me know about it."

"I will do that."

"And senator, one more thing."

"Yes?"

"If Arjun Azmi or his people push to close that contract, can you stall them? At least for a few weeks until I get to the bottom of this."

"With pleasure. Arjun and his wife Lalita are acting with a presumption I would like to cool."

"Thank you senator. This has been very helpful."

Detective Abbott stared at his black armband after the phone call. He was no longer seething. He was putting the pieces together. He punched his desk intercom button. "Please tell Detective Reed I'm free."

A blonde young woman darkened his doorway. "Yes?"

"Detective Reed, what do we know about Hank Rudzinski?"

"Please call me Bonnie. I am so sorry about Delgado."

"Me too. Let's find his killers."

"Your question about Hank Rudzinski is a good one."

"What do you mean?"

"We've been monitoring his smartphone location for the last three days. His smartphone has been at his work location and now is in the Lake Tahoe area."

"Are you saying he separated from his smartphone?"

"Our security camera captures show him getting into his company delivery van at the Costco at Kifer Road and Lawrence Expressway. He left his smartphone at work during that time. It took a while for the facial recognition team to find this gem."

"When? When was he at Costco with this delivery van?"

"Two days ago."

"Two days ago? He procured supplies for his friends."

"We've confirmed that Jiao Liu and Jake Hawes are not with him at Lake Tahoe."

"Bring him in for questioning."

"It may take a while."

"Is he running?"

"No."

"Bring him in as soon as you can."

"Will do. Again, I'm sorry about Detective Delgado."

"Thank you." Abbott watched the young detective leave. At Delgado's funeral, he blamed himself for letting his partner meet a potential killer alone. But with this new ACES Corporation and Senator Gita Bhatt information, he sought blame elsewhere. A seventy-eight billion dollar contract was a hell of a lot more likely motive for murder than a love triangle.

27

Jake opened his eyes and lifted his head. "Ow." He focused on his surroundings. He pulled the sleeping bag off his shoulder and remembered. After eating two microwave dinners and drinking a gallon of water and green tea, his exhaustion forced sleep.

"Stop being a baby. I got all the metal out of your back. You're going to be fine." Jiao was across the florescent lit conference room sitting on one of the two breakroom chairs. She used the other chair as a desk. She was hunched, staring at a tablet on the left and making notes on the legal pad on her right.

Jake looked at her. "I'm still recovering and I was shot."

"You ate half our food and slept four hours. We've got work to do."

Jake got up, and gingerly lifted his right arm. "You're right. This isn't as bad. Your luggage strap bandage saved me."

"We're not saved yet."

Jake crossed the room and used his good arm to hug Jiao. "What did you find in the pictures from our nighttime activity?"

"We both captured the same two men. One wore a light colored pink blazer."

"Pink – that's what that color was."

"We have these two men at both the guesthouse of the Azmi mansion and later at the old semiconductor fab next to the ACES Corporation campus."

"Old semiconductor fab?"

"You were smart to take that video."

"What did it show?"

"There were some words I picked out of the conversation. They talked about a desi mal shipment and I believe one said Amrish was a gaandu." She looked up at Jake. "Gaandu is the Hindi word for asshole."

"And who is Desi Mal?"

"Desi mal could be a name but they talk about a desi mal shipment. It took me a while to figure it out but desi mal is also what the locals in Mumbai call heroin."

"Heroin? How does that tie into our Holy Grail of energy storage?"

Jiao set the tablet down and leaned back in her seat. "This is so big. In India, and the rest of Asia, families are everything. They cluster together in business, government, and in crime." She turned to Jake. "Sometimes all three are connected."

Jake leaned his good shoulder against the wall. "So we're up against an international group involved in the opiate epidemic as well as the state's renewable energy contracts?"

"Yes. We looked in the right place."

"Yeah, these bastards have armed drones and aren't afraid to use them in Los Altos Hills."

"The Azmis also knew you and Detective Delgado were meeting for breakfast."

"Let me heat up some water so I can make coffee."

"Green tea will be better for you. It'll wake you up and help you heal."

"So you are worried about me."

"Of course but we need to plan."

The two went to the door. Jiao flicked off the conference room light. They went into the breakroom. Jake saw it was mid-day. "You want a plan to go after the Azmis when we just found out they're one of the biggest and baddest international crime families in California?"

Jiao filled two mugs with water and put them in the microwave. She set the time for ninety seconds and turned to Jake. "What did you say about the value of their character?"

"I said their character is the same value as dog shit that I scrape off the bottom of my shoe."

"Well, they're bigger. So this is like elephant shit we're scrapping off our shoes." She turned at the microwave bell, extracted the mugs, and plopped in two tea bags.

"I'm not sure you're using that comparison right."

Jiao laughed and handed Jake the steaming mug. "Regardless, we're stepping in shit."

Jake laughed and snagged another breakroom chair as the two went back to the conference room. He sat beside Jiao and sipped the tea. "This is good." He noted a line drawing on Jiao's legal pad. "What's that?"

"I made a mind map of what we're facing."

"A mind map?"

"Yes, I'm showing all the connections of the ideas and people."

Jake took another sip as he stared at the diagram. "Why do you have a star beside Detective Abbott's name?"

"I think he'll be able to help us."

"Why?"

"Because he's part of one of the most computer savvy departments in the country. By now, he knows that both Arjun and the ACES Corporation are involved." She picked up the mind map. "By now, he knows State Senator Gita Bhatt is involved."

"How is the senator involved?"

"She is heading California's renewable energy efforts."

"That's why Amrish sent her the email."

"And by now, Detective Abbott knows Arjun is threatening you, me, and Hank."

"Hank?"

"That was on the text you received before meeting Detective Delgado."

"That's right." Jake drank more of the rejuvenating green tea. He nodded. "Did we capture anything else from the tablet pictures?"

"I got the license plate numbers of two cars including the one the man in the pink blazer drove."

Jake nodded. "That's good. We should get this to Detective Abbott."

"There's more. I discovered Amrish blind copied Indira Cheena on a couple of emails."

Jake paused before asking about the relationship. He knew Amrish was previously married or maybe he was still married. He cleared his throat. "Who's Indira Cheena?"

"Indira is Amrish's sister and she lives in San Francisco working for the social media company, Parivara."

"His sister?"

"I did a search on her. She's quite skilled in software programming."

"When did you have time to do all this?"

"When you were sleeping under an overpass, I was working."

"Good work too. Amrish has a sister in San Francisco named Indira. That's really something. I wonder if she's a hacker. I wonder if she knows about the Azmis."

"Probably."

Jake stared at the mind map. "We should get all this new information to Detective Abbott." He nodded. "And we should go to San Francisco and track Indira down."

Jiao turned and fixed Jake in a steady gaze. "You want to leave our safe hideout and go to San Francisco?"

"Yes. We can buy Caltrain tickets with cash."

"Caltrain?"

"It goes into the heart of the city. I took the train with friends a couple of times to watch Giants baseball games. Going to the city at night on the last Caltrain run is perfect."

"Are you sure the ticket machine takes cash?"

"I am. It probably has a camera so we'll need to cover that as we walk up. But it does take cash."

"Wait a minute. I agree with getting all this information to Detective Abbott but what would we do in San Francisco?"

"We find Indira and lay everything out for her. We tell her that the only way her brother's death means something is if we get his philosopher's stone patent out in the world."

Jiao looked around the conference room. "We have the last of our stuff here."

"We can take roller bags onto the train. And we'll take our sleeping bags."

She pointed to the mind map. "What about everything we've found? How do we get this to Detective Abbott?"

Jake looked at the tablet, USB drives, and legal pads. He smiled. "We'll tell Hank to lead Detective Abbott here."

"You don't think that's pulling Hank in too deep?"

"It's like you said. Detective Abbott is part of the most technically savvy police department in the country. They have my smartphone and saw the texted threat to me, you, and Hank. They could be talking to Hank now."

"Hank said he was going to Lake Tahoe for a couple of days."

"That's right." Jake rubbed his chin. "The timing works. Hank can help the police by leading them here."

"I'll organize our evidence for them to discover."

"Yes." Jake looked around. "We should pack."

"Let's clean up first. I need to get you a clean bandage."

"Good point. Do you know where Indira Cheena lives?"

"No, I know the address of where she works but not where she lives."

"San Francisco has crazy high housing costs. Are you sure she lives in the city?"

"Yes, she put it in her background and complained about being poor on what would be a high salary any place else in the country."

"Let's get cleaned up. We're going to the city."

28

Hank Rudzinski drove on Highway 50, late in the evening, through the Sierras toward Sacramento with his wife, Amy, beside him. He looked over and saw she was fuming.

"I can't believe you kept this from me."

"It was better that way. Jake and Jiao are good friends of mine. You remember Jake from the army socials."

"I remember he was married at the time. So Jake got divorced and now he's shacking up with this Jiao girl. They're both on the run and you're helping them."

"We help each other."

"The police want to talk to you. Did his helping you ever lead to police involvement? I can't believe this. You helped two fugitives suspected of murder escape."

"I helped them hide to find answers. There is no escape."

"The police are going to put you in jail. What are we supposed to tell Michael?"

"Michael's fine and . . ." The vehicle's Bluetooth connection showed his phone was ringing. Hank used a firm voice to activate the hands free device. "Answer."

"Hank, this is Jake." The voice of his friend came over the SUV's speakers. A tinge of desperation was apparent in Jake's tone. "I'm using one of those burner phones."

"Jake, I'm driving back from Tahoe. I'm going to be talking to the police in a couple hours."

"Good, I want you to take them to our hiding place."

"Why? Will you be there?"

"No, we're not there now but Jiao and I collected evidence and left it for them."

"You found out who did this?" Hank tried to be vague. Jake's phone may be a burner but his wasn't.

"Yes and Hank stay away from this thing. I got shot in the back from an armed drone. We are up against some bad dudes."

Hank's eyebrows rose at his friend's description of his enemies. Jake was a fellow Desert Storm veteran who stood beside Hank amidst vast carnage when their army unit, the 13th Infantry Division, destroyed a portion of the Iraqi Republican Guards. They both knew evil and the slippery slope one went down when meeting it. "You got shot in the back and are still going after these guys?"

"I'll live. Jiao patched me up. We have to finish this fight. The information we left for the police will help."

Amy grunted in disgust at the speakerphone conversation. Hank shook his head. "Jake, if these guys are that bad and you have evidence, let the police take it from here."

"Hank, these guys are into murder, heroin, weapons, blackmail, bribes, state government corruption – they are pure evil. Even worse, I think they have someone in the police department."

Hank hoped this call was being recorded. "And you want me to lead them to your evidence?"

"We think Detective Abbott is a good guy. Is that who contacted you?"

"Yes but it wasn't a pleasant conversation." He paused. "Jake, you're really going after these guys?"

"There's a couple more pieces we have to put together. I have no choice. We used to talk about the burdens of character. This is one of them. Duty dictates I see this through."

That was the old Jake Hank knew from the 13th Infantry Division. "I admire your conviction. We could use more character like that in today's world. Jake, I'll take the police to your hideout but listen, you remember our talks about our killing demons?"

"What?" Amy asked.

"Yes I do Hank." Jake either didn't hear Amy or chose not to.

"The burdens of character can get you into tough spots. If one of those evil guys get too close, don't hesitate. Let your killing demon out of his cage."

"That's good advice. I will."

"Good luck Jake. Tell Jiao I wish you both good luck."

"Will do. You led us through the minefield in the desert but, like you said, this is my minefield. I won't bother you again until this is all over."

"Good luck Jake," Amy said giving her husband a sidelong glance.

Hank and Detective Abbott stood in the vacant office building that served as Jake and Jiao's hideout the last three days. They found two full but tied off garbage bags of trash in the breakroom. Hank winced when the detective ordered the contents of the garbage analyzed. On a chair in a vacant conference room they found a tablet, USB drive, and yellow legal pad.

Abbott picked up the pad with his gloved hand and pointed to a diagram. "What do you know about this?"

"It's a mind map. Jake and Jiao are showing you the connections they've found."

The detective turned the pad over, covering the writing. "What do you know about those connections?"

"I know this has something to do with an energy storage patent. Energy storage has been the Holy Grail quest of the renewable energy industry for decades."

"And what do you know about the people supposedly framing Jake Hawes and Doctor Jiao Liu?"

"Nothing other than they're evil."

"You risked life imprisonment by helping Jake and Jiao and you don't know what they found?"

"Jake and I served in combat together. I trust him."

Detective Abbott nodded. The detective was also a military veteran and he understood that type of trust. "Do you have any idea where they're going now?"

"I don't. Jake wanted it that way. He was shot in the back from an armed drone. He wanted to distance me from this fight."

"Did he say where he was when he was attacked by this illegal drone?"

"No. Whatever they wanted shared, they left for you here."

"You should have told him to turn himself in."

"I did. He believes someone in the police department is compromised. Jake thinks they need more information."

"And he thinks he and his girlfriend can get it?"

Hank considered the girlfriend comment. He glanced around the conference room and surmised that Jake and Jiao did rekindle their romance. He turned back to the detective. "I wouldn't bet against them but they're fighting powerful enemies."

The detective narrowed his eyes. "You want me to believe they're fighting powerful enemies that not only kill but are also framing your friends."

"I do." Hank pointed to the legal pad. "They tried to explain that." He cleared his throat. "Am I under arrest?"

"I could throw you in jail right now." Detective Abbott glared at him. "But I'll use the fact you took us to their hiding place as an act of good faith. You can go but no more trips to Tahoe. You are on a very short string."

"Thank you. Detective Abbott . . . get the bastards that are killing people and framing my friends."

Jake and Jiao got off the last Caltrain stop at the San Francisco 4th and King Street station just past midnight. They were deep in the city. They were amped during the trip from the excitement. The fear of being captured heightened their senses.

Hours earlier Jake and Jiao packed their bags with clothes and food, attached their sleeping bags to their roller luggage, and walked seven blocks from their Arques Avenue hiding place up Lawrence Expressway to the Caltrain station at San Zeno Way just across from the Costco Hank used to get them supplies.

Every person they saw prompted fear-induced excitement. Seeing either an enemy or well-meaning friend would mean capture. A block from the station, Jake called Hank and told him to take the police to their hideout. That call sealed the deal. There was no turning back. Their safe and undiscovered haven would be crawling with police.

Jake tried to be nonchalant in covering the ticket station camera as Jiao used her cash to buy two three-zone tickets. He hoped they kept themselves hidden. It was a cliché that the police would be monitoring all modes of transportation. Their enemies' reach was such that they could be watching as well. The only way their plan to visit Indira Cheena worked is if they didn't get caught. Both Jiao and Jake felt two invisible hands closing in on them – one from their enemies and one from the police. If either caught them, the game would be up.

By the time Jake and Jiao got off the train, they were weary. It was going to get cold at night in San Francisco. They needed warmth and a place to hide. Both those needs were unmet as they left the train platform. But they were in a city teeming with people. They were in a city teeming with homeless. They planned to blend in and hide here but first, they moved with purpose from the Caltrain station.

"What street?" Jake asked.

"Townsend," Jiao replied. "We need to go up Townsend."

The two walked out of the Caltrain station and into the drizzling rain of San Francisco pulling their roller luggage behind them. It was cold, wet, and dark. They both, in the past, had seen the affluent side of the bright city many times. They were about to see the other side.

Jake wondered as they walked block by block up Townsend if the homeless shelter could accommodate them for a night. It had to. They were running out of money, time, and options. At a roundabout five blocks from the station they angled left on Henry Adams Street. Three blocks later they went right on 16th Street.

As they went under Highway 101 Jake's heart sank. He'd hoped the 101 underpass would provide possibility of shelter much as the Homestead – Interstate 85 overpass had during his escape from the Azmi mansion. But no such luck. Highway 101 was so high above the street there were no embankments or safe hiding places.

The two walked over a mile up 16th Street saying little as cold drizzle soaked them. Jake shivered and seriously wondered if hypothermia would end their quest. He looked at Jiao. Her jaw was set in the determined expression he'd seen so often when she was solving a complex technical problem. He loved Jiao and wished there was a way to spare her this agony. They made a right off 16th Street onto Wiese Street and, after a block, made a right and walked up to the Episcopal Community Services shelter. They stopped for a moment at the sign: San Francisco Navigation Center, Street to Home.

"I hope this works," Jiao said.

"Their website talked about being the Good Samaritan. We need a Good Samaritan about now."

"This is the last address we looked up. We know this place and where Indira works."

They stood there hoping that at 1:30 a.m. someone would come out and welcome them. "I've got thirty dollars to my name. How much money do you have left?" Jake asked.

"I've got a hundred and twenty dollars. That's it."

Jake shuddered. "We're both soaked. They have to take us. We can't sleep on the street."

The night shift clerk wasn't happy about being rousted at that time but, taking one look at the drenched forlorn couple, took pity on them. Jake signed them in as Mister and Mrs. Jones. They were set up in a large room that had a couple spare bed spaces. The bed spaces were constructed of welded thick sheet metal painted slate grey. It wasn't the best situation as their sleeping bags were damp, but they were out of the rain. They had a chance. It was a slim chance to be sure, but both were relieved to be in the shelter.

They'd staked everything on this San Francisco trip. Both Jake and Jiao knew they had one day left to find answers. They were almost out of money and almost out of time.

29

The day shift San Francisco Navigation Center manager wasn't happy with their two new guests and insisted on identification. Jake and Jiao thanked the woman for the evening's shelter and, for the first time since Detective Delgado's murder, went outside in broad daylight. They departed dragging their roller luggage which were bulky with attached sleeping bags. Jake noticed cameras everywhere. *I'll bet*, Jake thought, *the Navigation Center manager calls the police and notifies them of the strange couple that spent the night.* There was no place they would be safe for long.

The evening of travel and rain had taken its toll. The couple looked much like the homeless they left behind in the shelter. In many ways, they were worse. They had police searching for them as murderers and their enemies – the real murderers – wanted to kill them. Jake feared their bold plan was unwinding into an impossible situation.

"What now?" Jiao asked. She stared at the San Francisco Navigation Center, Street to Home sign.

"Let's get away from this shelter. The desk camera captured our image and the desk clerk may have called the police."

"Okay." Jiao's weariness was apparent.

The two left the Navigation Center. They went left on 16th Street and then turned left onto Mission Street. "This will take us into the right part of the city," Jake said. He looked at Jiao's dogged expression and felt a pang. "We'll find a place to eat."

As Jake and Jiao pulled their roller luggage down Mission Street they discovered others like them. They had stumbled on a method the San Francisco homeless were using – pulling luggage with an attached sleeping bag. Like others on the street, they mingled with those in suits. They stuck to the groups of homeless carrying backpacks and pulling roller bags. If observers looked close, they would note that Jake and Jiao didn't fit in with their upscale clothes. But no one made eye contact with the couple as they pulled their luggage behind them like so many of the homeless.

They walked several blocks, went under Highway 101, and continued on Mission. It wasn't raining but it was cool and overcast. The movement kept them warm. They stopped and looked at a taco truck named Taqueria Cazadores. "This looks good," Jake said.

"I want to sit down and eat. We should go further." Jiao wasn't happy but she was as determined as Jake to see this through.

Three blocks later they saw a Peet's Coffee shop but decided they needed more substantial food. They considered Moya, an Ethiopian restaurant at 9th Street but again, decided to keep going. "Maybe we should've stopped at that food truck," Jake said.

"There's a lot of restaurants," Jiao replied. "We'll find the right one."

At 7th Street they saw the Tēo Restaurant and Bar but decided it was too visible. They pondered going into the Subway Restaurant but then Jiao noticed a combination Vietnamese and Chinese restaurant. More from fatigue then the perfect choice, they decided to stop at the 7 Mission Restaurant. The couple found a booth. They piled their luggage on one side and sat next to each other shoulder to shoulder on the opposite side. They weren't hidden but, in the teeming city of San Francisco, figured the 7 Mission Restaurant was as good a place to eat as any.

The small restaurant served over a hundred menu selections. Jiao and Jake both opted for items from the fried rice part of the menu. Jiao got the shrimp fried rice and Jake, never one to be too adventurous with Asian food, got the chicken fried rice. They decided to split an egg roll as the final touch.

The food and atmosphere provided the couple a calm respite. They ate their food with water and green tea. The nourishment and relaxation revitalized them. "This was a good pick," Jake said. "I didn't see any cameras."

"We're only a few blocks away from Parivara – where Indira works."

Jake took a mouthful of food and washed it down with a sip of water. "This is just what we needed. I think . . ." He stopped and turned at the sound of a siren. He and Jiao waited while the siren sound rose to a crescendo and then dulled. "Whew, I'm jumpy."

"What were you going to say?"

"I think after we meet Indira, you should turn yourself in."

"And what – throw myself on the mercy of the law? I don't think so."

"Hank would have led Detective Abbott to our Sunnyvale hideout by now. They have everything we've found."

"The evidence and links I drew on that mind map are still too thin a tie to Amrish. Connected people like the Azmis get all kinds of emails. They might even say they've been hacked. We need more information."

"You're saying we need a stronger tie between Amrish and Arjun."

"And the energy storage patent. There's more to this than we've found."

Jake looked at the far wall. "Then Indira is our last hope." His eyes focused on the large television screen at the back of the restaurant. A television news announcer was in front of a familiar building and saying something Jake couldn't hear. "That building on TV . . ."

Jiao turned and looked. "That's the Navigation Center. Maybe they turned us in." Those words no sooner left Jiao's mouth when the screen flashed to side by side pictures of Jake and Jiao.

Their server was staring at the screen and, when their pictures were shown, put her hand to her mouth and groaned. She put a smartphone to her ear and turned to the couple sitting in the booth.

"We need to go, now!" Jake jumped out of the booth.

The two left the restaurant in a rush. "Our bags are back there," Jiao said. They paused for a moment but the increasing sound of sirens spurred them to move across and down the street.

They went a half a block away and watched the entrance to the 7 Mission Restaurant from Howard Street. "I can run back and get them," Jake said. A police car with flashing lights screeched to a stop next to their restaurant. "No way."

212

"Someone must have called before that news story."

"The clerk at the Navigation Center got them on our trail. Let's move." The two jogged up Howard Street and peeled into a small park. They went to the far side, mingled with the tents and other homeless in the park, and leaned up against a large tree. A light drizzle of rain coated them.

"My tablet and USB sticks are in my bag," Jiao said.

"And two of the burner phones are in mine." Jake felt inside his jacket pocket. "I have one left."

Jiao shook her head. "This isn't working. Every time we move, things get worse." She looked at Jake and whispered. "We are fugitives suspected of murder. The police will shoot us when they see us."

The drizzle turned to rain. Jake shuddered and stared at Jiao. "We came all this way." He listened for sirens but heard nothing. The groups of people using the park as a tent village must've saw Jake and Jiao as kindred spirits in a similar predicament. The homeless paid little attention to the soaked couple.

"This place seems hidden," Jiao said.

"Maybe we wait here until 5 p.m. and then try to find Indira."

A dog barked. Jake snapped his head toward the sound. "Would they put a K-9 unit on us?"

"They could. They have our luggage and could use it to get the dogs after our scent." Another dog barked.

"We need to move."

Jake and Jiao exited the small park on Langton Street and moved south. They got to Harrison Street and took a right. Again, even close to the posh part of the city, they were able to blend in with numerous homeless. There was something that did make them stand out – the homeless were better equipped for the cold rain.

They followed Harrison Street to 8th Street and turned left. There was a small copse of trees and they meandered around the ever present tents and sought shelter under the trees. Jake saw Jiao shiver and he pulled her close. He then shivered and she wrapped her arms around him. Blocks away sirens blared and dogs barked. The rain eased but by now they were soaked through and bitterly cold. "Let's go to Indira's company, Parivara." Jake said. He was desperate. "If we get caught, let's get caught there."

"What good will that do?"

"We made it all the way to San Francisco, we should try." He looked around. "What's the best way to get there?"

"Parivara is next to Twitter."

"That's right, we should follow Harrison to 11th Street. We'll make a big loop."

"But it's too early. There'll be cameras everywhere looking for our faces."

"And we can't go in the front door of Parivara, that's for sure."

The sound of dogs barking prompted them to move again. They followed Harrison to 11th Street. They didn't have a plan, they were moving on instinct and desperation. They made a right on 11th and moved block up to Folsom Street. Sirens blared of approaching police. "This is folly." Jake said.

"They're searching our bags and that's good."

"Why is that good?"

"I left another evidence pack in one that includes the same mind map I left for Detective Abbott. Let's keep moving."

Jake didn't have a better idea. The couple walked three blocks in the drizzle, shivering in silence. They crossed Mission and moved toward Market Street. "There's the Uber headquarters. We're almost there."

Among those with umbrellas, a woman, head down with a hooded rain jacket, rushed down 11th Street toward them. She got up to them and stopped. "Jiao! Come with me."

Jake and Jiao froze at the recognition. The woman was young with an earnest expressive face. "Indira?"

"Both of you, come with me now."

The three linked arms and Indira pulled them down 11th back in the direction they had come. They made a left on Mission, walked four blocks at the pace of a jog, and came to a small apartment complex. "Keep your heads down," Indira said as she unlocked the front door. The three went upstairs and in moments stood dripping in a studio apartment.

"Indira Cheena?" Jake couldn't believe what just happened.

"Yes and it's about time you came here."

30

Jake felt the warmth of the studio apartment and smiled. The well furnished apartment offered a great view of the city. He looked at Amrish's sister. "We were on our last legs. You were expecting us?"

"Ever since you fell off the map." Indira was all business. "You two need to get out of those wet clothes. We've got things to discuss."

"How did you know we'd be here?" Jiao asked.

"You two are famous. Your pictures were all over the news this morning. When I heard the Navigation Center flagged your presence in the city, I guessed you were coming to find me."

"Amrish told you about us." Jake peeled off his jacket. "Did he tell you about the patent?"

Indira laughed. "That's all he talked about. He wanted to democratize the evolution of that storage device."

"Really?" Jake realized he had Amrish wrong. His anger at his old boss was misplaced. "How?"

"Maker spaces. Amrish was contriving energy storage building kits for kids to experiment with at maker spaces. He viewed it like the old Heath kits from the early computer days. He wanted everyone to get involved at solving the energy problem, at solving climate change."

Jake stared at Indira. "That's a noble quest."

Jiao nodded. "But why did he push Jake and me away from him? We would've helped." She removed her jacket and shoes. She shivered. "I do need to get dry."

"I'll lay out some clothes. You should take a hot shower." Indira turned to Jake. "I'll give you a robe to wear and put your wet stuff in the dryer."

"That'd be great."

"Amrish found the old patent by trolling for the ACES Corporation. ACES had the strategy of locking up expired patent technology by tweaking prior art and reapplying for a new patent. They're doing that to stop competition." She looked from one to the other. "You do know about ACES, right?"

"Yes, we do."

"ACES Corporation is run by the Azmis, what looks like a reputable, successful family but is rotten to the core."

"We knew that too." Jiao smiled. "I am freezing. Is your shower this way?"

"I'll show you." Indira escorted Jiao to her bathroom. She returned and fixed Jake with a quizzical look. "Are you two together?"

"Um . . . yeah, we are."

"I thought Amrish and Jiao were together."

"They were after Jiao and I broke up. Then he pushed her away. By the way, I heard Amrish was married."

"Hmm . . . yes, it was a loveless arranged marriage from years ago."

"Arranged marriage? In this day and age?"

"Change is slower than anyone wants." She looked toward the shower. "Amrish was conflicted about his family in India but he did love Jiao."

"So do I."

"Amrish wanted to get her out of harm's way. It was only two months ago that Amrish found out who he was dealing with."

"You mean that the Azmi's are snakes in the grass?"

"They're worse than that. They are Brahman devils that act above the law." She glared at Jake. "They killed my brother. I hoped you'd come to me. I wasn't going to go to the police with my information unless you got caught. I'm glad you found me. The Azmis' reach is such they'd have silenced me if I told anyone about the patent. I don't want to die."

"Thank you for looking for us," Jake replied. "We were desperate. Jiao and I both want to avenge your brother. I had no idea about the secrets he was hiding." He noticed that Indira was wearing a blouse with similar buttons to a men's shirt. "You should take off that blouse."

"What?"

"Your brother was killed by an exploding shirt button that looked a lot like the ones on that blouse."

"I didn't know that." Indira unbuttoned and removed her blouse. "Is that what happened to the detective in Sunnyvale?"

"Yes." Jake's attention was arrested by Indira's smooth skin and mauve lacy bra.

"Okay Jake, your turn." Jiao came into the studio's living room wearing the clothes Indira laid out. She saw Indira in only a bra and stopped. "Am I missing something?"

"Jake told me about the exploding button. You better get that blouse off as well."

"That's right." Jiao removed her blouse revealing a white lacy bra.

Jake gaped. Two fit exotic women who were also whip smart and of high character nonchalantly lounged in front of him. In spite of all of his troubles, he found the view the height of sexuality. He stood. "I'm getting a shower."

"Leave your wet clothes by the door so I can put them in the dryer." Indira walked to her closet. "I'll get you a robe."

"Thanks." Jake walked to the bathroom and turned for one more view of the sexy pair. "You two put some clothes on." He heard the women laugh as he entered the bathroom. He winced when he took his shirt off. "Jiao, I need help."

Jiao and Indira came to the bathroom. Indira gaped wide-eyed at Jake's bloody bandage held on by luggage straps. "What happened?" Indira asked.

"The Azmis," Jiao replied. "I almost forgot about that." Jiao came behind Jake and released the straps. "This may sting a bit." Jake tensed in pain as Jiao peeled the washcloth off his wound.

"The Azmis did this?" Indira asked.

"I went to the Azmi mansion and they sent an armed drone after me."

"You got shot by a drone?"

"In a cemetery – the same cemetery that Steve Jobs is buried at if you can believe it. Ow."

"Okay, get cleaned up," Jiao said. We'll find something to use as a bandage when you're done."

The shower felt like a burst of warm heaven splashing on his body. He washed off days of accumulated dirt and perspiration. He realized the last time he had a shower was in the Sunnyvale Residence Inn just before they went into hiding. He soaked up the heat and let the hot water spray his sore wound. He dried himself with a plush towel.

Jake marveled how cherished taken-for-granted things became after only days without them. Getting clean in a hot shower lifted his spirits. Things were in a much better state. Indira finding them was a godsend. He came out of the shower wrapped in a towel and stopped by the sinks. "Jiao, do you want to look at this wound."

Both women, now sporting sweatshirts, came to the bathroom. Jake felt exquisite vulnerability being wrapped in nothing but a towel as Jiao and Indira examined his wound.

"I can't believe they were so brazen to shoot you with a drone," Indira said. "This proves everything I've found out about the Azmis."

Jiao dabbed his wound. Jake groaned and clutched his towel. "We dug up some information but I got shot doing it," Jake said. "What did you find out about the Azmis?"

"Amrish started me on the trail. Arjun got him believing in changing the world through renewable energy both here and in India. When Amrish found the old high temperature superconductor storage patent he realized that today's technology makes it practical. Amrish got the maker space idea from a Leo Laporte show."

"Leo Laporte? That name's familiar."

"Amrish saw a special Leo did on maker spaces on the New Screen Savers."

"The Screen Savers – that's where I know Leo from." Jake tried to keep his mind off the throbbing pain in his back as Jiao kept cleaning. "I didn't know The Screen Savers was still on."

"It's a web streamed show now. Anyway, Leo did a New Screen Savers' special on the San Mateo Maker Space about the same time Amrish discovered the 1980s Department of Energy patent. I don't know how well you knew my brother but after he saw that maker space special, he was on a mission."

"Amrish was right," Jiao said. "If there was a kit that people could use to store their household electricity, everybody would want one."

"Tell me about these maker spaces," Jake said.

"They're like engineering labs for kids. They have 3D printers, Raspberry Pi and Arduino controllers, table top mills, you name it." The dryer beeped behind her. "You're clothes are dry."

"Great."

Indira departed and Jiao applied antibiotic salve and placed a clean wash rag over the wide wound. "I think this Ace bandage will work better than my luggage strap to hold it in place."

Indira returned with a bundle of clothes. "Amrish wanted every smart kid to be working on this storage device. Maker spaces are hooked into crowdfunding sites like Kickstarter or StartEngine. People would've invested in the best designs and storage companies would've popped up all around the country."

Jake took the bundle of clothes. "Your brother was a good man."

"That's why the Azmis killed him."

Jake went into the shower, closed the door, and reveled as he dressed in his dryer-fresh warm clothes. He returned to the living room with a wide grin. "It's hard to describe how good that felt."

"I agree," Jiao said. She smiled at Jake. "You look like a new man."

"I feel like a new man."

Jiao turned to Indira. "I still don't get it. The ACES Corporation has all the California renewable energy contracts. Arjun Azmi and his family are well connected. Why risk everything to stop Amrish?"

Indira's face darkened. "Arjun and his wife Lalita have a grand plan. It's almost hard to believe. Jake's wound shows us just how far they're willing to go."

"How big is the Arjun and Lalita group?"

"It's actually direct family and cousins. Amrish and I were able to come up with forty-three both here and in India."

"It sounds like a mafia family."

"It's something like that. Arjun and Lalita have two sons and two daughters. They're already lining them up to get into politics. Arjun and Lalita are big political donors. They're getting most of their renewable energy contracts lined up through State Senator Gita Bhatt."

"That's explains Amrish's email. But why wouldn't the Azmis pitch the storage patent to Senator Bhatt?"

"Hiding the energy storage patent was part of the Azmi grand plan. Arjun wanted to squelch the storage patent in California and use it to set up a company headed by his brother in India. He wanted India to own that power."

Jake sat on the edge of his chair. "With all the connections in California and the U.S., why double down on India? Family?"

"In twenty years India will surpass China and be the world's largest economy."

"Really?"

"Besides, the Azmi family are Brahmans who were tight with the British when they ruled India. They've been trying to get back into power there ever since the British left."

"What kind of bizarre plan is that?"

"It's not so bizarre. The caste system is in Arjun and Lalita's blood. They feel they should be on top – that they're entitled to rule. They are taking steps in both the U.S. and India to secure their position."

"The caste system's driving them? I'm glad we don't have a caste system in the U.S." Jake said.

Indira and Jiao exchanged a glance and laughed.

"What?"

"Never mind." Indira continued. "Amrish and I found out the Azmis also have a pharmaceutical concern as an offshoot to their Hong Kong parent corporation."

"Pharmaceutical?"

"They're using that to bring in opiates, heroin."

"Desi mal," Jiao said.

Indira nodded.

"That's a hell of a plan," Jake said. "The Azmis want business and political empires in both the U.S. and India. They use drugs to fund their activities and view their renewable energy contracts in California as a key stepping stone."

"And Arjun wants to give the storage patent to his brother in India to give him the glory and stop California and the U.S. from leading in energy storage," Jiao said.

"That's why Amrish wanted to stop them," Jake said.

"Amrish figured all that out but missed one important thing. It wasn't until just weeks ago that Amrish found out Lalita's brother, Laksh, is their muscle. Laksh does the killing." Indira sighed. "He's nasty in ways you could only imagine. Laksh was even accused of poaching tigers in India."

"Laksh has a lot of help," Jiao said. "I saw it in Santa Clara. Those RF-triggered exploding buttons weren't trivial to make."

"Laksh is here in San Francisco looking for you two."

Jake's eyes widened. "What? How do you know?"

"I went to the Navigation Center this morning to see if I could find you and I saw Laksh. He thinks he's a fashion expert and walks around in a pink blazer."

Jake and Jiao exchanged a glance. "Laksh is the one who wears the pink blazer? We both saw him as well."

"There's nothing he won't do. If he's here looking for you, you are in grave danger."

"What about you?"

"Amrish had me be very careful and, through my social media site Parivara, be very visible. That's why I kept all this Azmi information to myself. That's why I went looking for you two when I heard you came to San Francisco." Indira looked from Jiao to Jake. "If Laksh stops you, it's all over. They'll quash the investigation and Arjun and Lalita will have free reign."

"The energy storage patent will stay hidden," Jake said.

"How would we stop them?" Jiao asked.

"To stop them we have to stop Laksh," Jake said. "He's the key. If we tag Laksh as doing the killing for the Azmis, their whole plan unwinds."

"You'll need my information," Indira said.

"What information?" Jiao asked.

"I have the patent detail and references. I also have a maker space kit design Amrish wanted to release. He blind copied Senator Bhatt on some of his emails to Arjun. I have those emails." Indira nodded. "I have all the information we dug up on the Azmis and Laksh these past two months."

"If we shed light on all these secrets, the Azmi family is ruined." Jiao nodded.

"It's funny how secrets protect the evil more than the innocent," Jake said.

Indira rose and went to her computer. She picked up two USB thumb drives. "I put everything I have on these."

Jake took one and Jiao took the other. "If we can show Laksh for what he is . . ."

"With this information and what we provided the police yesterday," Jiao continued, "we can bring this whole thing down on them."

"We need more," Jake said. "We need to get Laksh in a vulnerable position."

"Amrish met him and managed to get his mobile number a couple months ago. It may not have changed." Indira pulled out a laptop and extended it to Jiao. "Take this Chromebook, there's free Wi-Fi all over the city. It could help."

Jake looked at the USB thumb drive in his hand, lifted his head, and locked eyes with Jiao. "Let's take the Azmis down."

Part IV

Confrontation

31

Jake and Jiao left Indira and began their planned trek to Golden Gate Park. Indira had fed them and supplied them with a backpack to store the Chromebook, water, and energy bars. Jake tried to put on the backpack but was painfully reminded of his wound. Jiao shouldered the pack and they set off up Mission Street.

The two made a right on 9th Street and a left on Hayes Street. "Are you sure this is the way?" Jiao asked.

"Hayes Street will run us straight into the Golden Gate Park," Jake replied. "I didn't run on all those Bay to Breakers race teams for nothing."

Behind them a police cruiser drove by. Jiao watched it disappear around a corner. "That's probably the one headed to Indira's apartment."

"We were lucky Indira was warned," Jake said. "We barely got out of there."

"The police went first to Parivara to find her. It's a good thing one of her employees called and let her know."

The couple walked up what Jake remembered as the Hayes Street Hill part of the Bay to Breakers footrace. "If the police were set on her trail so was Laksh."

"Laksh scares me. He's the one who killed Amrish and Detective Delgado."

"We need to finish this," Jake replied. "Unless we get this information out, there's no other way."

They heard more sirens after they crossed Steiner Street. "Let's go in this park for a moment and I'll see if I can get Wi-Fi. I'd like to send Detective Abbott what Indira gave us. We left Indira's too fast to have a chance to look at all her information."

The couple went into a group of trees in what was Alamo Square Park and, again, saw a cluster of homeless tents. Jiao stopped and turned on the Chromebook. She waited. "I see a high school network but it's secured."

"Let's keep moving."

Jiao closed the laptop, put it in her pack, and shouldered the backpack. The two moved back to Hayes Street. "How did the police know to track down Indira?"

Jake marveled at Jiao's steady quick pace as much as her always thinking sharp mind. "Indira is Amrish's sister. It makes sense the police would talk to her." Their pace continued at its quick clip. "I don't think there're cameras to worry about here on Hayes Street."

"But why talk to Indira now? Why would they come the moment we're there?"

"Good question. I don't think it was coincidence."

"It's like they know our every move."

"Maybe but I don't think the Azmis have any idea of the information bomb Indira gave us. She found a lot of damaging stuff."

"I noticed you found Indira to be young and attractive."

"Jiao, I'm yours. You don't need to worry about that."

"Your eyes were popping out of your head when I came out of the shower."

"I'm a man, okay? And then when you took your blouse off, I was in hellish heaven."

"How men ever get anything done around women, I'll never know."

"It's our burden to carry."

Jiao laughed and Jake was warmed by the sound. "Let's talk about our plan once we get to Golden Gate Park."

"Once we get there, let's find a public Wi-Fi spot for you to send all this information to Detective Abbott. Between that information and what we left at the vacant office building, the detective should know we aren't the killers."

Jiao looked at the overcast sky. "I'm glad it stopped raining. I don't want to walk all around the park looking for a free Wi-Fi signal."

"I don't think it'll be hard to find a Wi-Fi network. I'll use my last burner phone to call Abbott. I have his card from the first interview. I'll tell him about Laksh."

"Do you tell him where we are?"

"That's the tricky part. I don't think so. We need to get Laksh into the park before the police. After talking to Abbott, I'll call Laksh at the number Indira gave us. I'll tell Laksh I have damaging information on the Azmi family and want to trade it."

"Trade it for what?"

"Doesn't matter. We just need him to take the bait."

"It does matter. We're trying to blackmail a known killer and we're in a secluded spot."

"We need the police to see that Laksh is involved. Bringing him to us will connect all the dots."

"Indira said Laksh was at the Navigation Center. He's looking for us. He's not looking to talk. He wants to kill us." Jiao walked at a faster pace. "We should've gotten Indira to send the email. They'll find the information anyway."

"We had to run out of Indira's apartment without fleshing all this out." Jake caught the concern and matched Jiao's quickened pace. "We should take Indira at her word that she won't offer the information by herself. It has to be us."

"Then after I send the email, we should call the police and let them handle it. This idea of getting the police to see Laksh is too risky. Indira and I ripped our shirts off for fear he'd kill us with a button."

Jake saw the point. Contacting Laksh was risky. "Let's get off the street and into the park. We need to think." The couple jogged the final three blocks and entered Golden Gate Park just north of the McLaren Lodge. "Let's get away from the parking lot," Jake said. They went into a small group of trees and moved north parallel to Stanyan Street. "No tents here."

"They're here," Jiao said. "They're just in the middle of the park. I can't believe how the homeless population exploded in this city the last few years."

"Wait, look at that." Jake pointed to a large ten story building along Stanyan Street.

Jiao stopped. "That's a hospital."

"Think there's a public Wi-Fi signal we can use?"

"Let's find out." Jiao shrugged out of her backpack and pulled out the Chromebook. She turned it on and looked at the Wi-Fi signals. "I see one labeled public."

"Good. Let's get this email sent and we'll be halfway there."

Jiao opened the internet browser. "I need to get onto my Gmail account." She pulled the USB stick out of her pocket and put it in the Chromebook. "This is a slow network."

Jake's attention was arrested by the squealing of tires. He looked up and saw that a black van stopped in front of them on Stanyan Street. He frowned and watched a door open. The man who got out of the passenger side wore a pink blazer. He grabbed Jiao's arm. "Run, it's Laksh."

"What?" She looked up and gasped. The man in the pink blazer hadn't seen them yet but was jogging into the park in their direction.

Jake and Jiao ran west deeper into the park as fast as they could go. Jake had grabbed the backpack and Jiao ran cradling the Chromebook. Jake was thankful for Jiao's speed. They ran up to the edge of the Conservatory Drive and went behind the Conservatory of Flowers. Jake and Jiao accelerated their pace as they crossed an open space and slowed once entering another group of trees. "Left, we need to turn." Jake steered them left and they sprinted across John F. Kennedy Drive and into another group of trees. Here, thankfully, they found clusters of tents.

They meandered around the tents and, for once, Jake was thankful for the San Francisco homeless problem. They stopped in the middle of the makeshift tent city. "Did you send the email?" Jake asked.

"No, I didn't have time." Jiao looked at the Chromebook. "I lost the USB drive too. It fell off during our run."

Jake's stomach tightened. *The Azmis are always a step ahead of us.* He forced calm. "I've got the other USB drive. There's enough memory on that Chromebook to copy the files."

Jiao looked around the tents. "Do you think he followed us into the park?"

"I don't know. It's a big place." He reached in his pocket and pulled out the USB drive Indira gave him. "See if you can copy these files to the Chromebook itself."

Jiao flicked open the screen and the Chromebook came to life. She stared at the internet browser notice. "We're too far away from that hospital network."

"We'll have to find another." He extended the USB drive to Jiao. "We're on the cusp of really taking it to the Azmis."

Jiao took the drive and plugged it into the Chromebook. "And Laksh is on the cusp of killing us." She tapped keys. "Okay, there's the files. I'll make a folder on the desktop and put them all in there."

Jake scanned the tent area. A few people were milling around but, after the rain, all were staying close to their setup shelters. *What happened to this great city?*

"There, all copied." Jiao extracted the USB drive and handed it to Jake.

"Good." He looked east as he pocketed the drive. "Do you hear that humming?"

Jiao followed Jake's gaze. "I do. What is that?"

"It sounds like . . ."

Two large drones, spaced a hundred yards apart, flew over John F. Kennedy Drive right toward them.

32

Detective Abbott fumed as he drove into San Francisco with his new partner, Detective Bonnie Reed. "Jake and Jiao are always one step ahead of us." He shook his head. "Their sighting in San Francisco should not have got to the news."

Detective Reed was working on her ruggedized police laptop from the passenger seat. "These two are smart and they are onto something. I'm amazed they linked ACES Corporation and the Azmi's to this murder."

"Murders," Abbott corrected. "My partner Delgado was killed by these guys."

"But who?" Reed asked. "Who is Arjun Azmi using to do the killing? Jiao and Jake's pictures show someone in a pink blazer at both sites. That was the one we heard in the video saying desi mal – India sourced heroin."

"If Jake and Jiao would have let us take them in, they'd be safe now."

"Those guys came here to meet Amrish's sister, Indira. They're putting the pieces together."

"Like I said, they are always a step ahead of us." Detective Abbott both cursed and admired the embattled couple. Being a U.S. Army veteran himself, Detective Abbott understood the dictates of duty and demands of character. He understood, more than his boss at police headquarters, why Hank helped his fellow soldier.

Detective Abbott was coming around to the idea, helped in no small part by the information Jake and Jiao left behind in Sunnyvale, that someone else was doing the killing. "The information they gathered and left for us at the vacant office building confirmed a lot of theories. We know about the storage device patent. We know about the ACES Corporation contracts and the Azmis political connections."

"And we know the Azmis have an illegal armed drone." Detective Reed tapped away at her computer. "We may know all that, but we still can't get warrants for ACES Corporation or the Azmis compound."

"How long?" If there was one thing Detective Abbott despised, it was elitist privilege, whether wielded through influence or money. In the case of Arjun and Lalita Azmi, it was both.

"The district attorney says it may take a week."

"They'll scrub those places clean in a week. How can the Azmis apply this much leverage?"

"They had their lawyers working the DA and judge before we even asked for warrants."

"This Amrish case makes me wonder."

"About what?"

"I wonder if we've gone backwards on basic justice."

"Political influence always plays a part. The Azmis donate to elected political leaders and they get their ear. When the state wants renewable energy contracts the big donors are first in line. It's the way things get done. There's always been a level of corruption in politics and contracts."

"This is different. This corruption covers a fifty year time span and seventy-eight billion dollars. This corruption involves murders. The Azmis are killing people and getting away with it."

"That's why Jiao and Jake are running. They can create reasonable doubt they didn't do the murders but don't have enough evidence on the Azmis."

"If it takes us a week to get warrants, we'll never get the evidence." Detective Abbot grimaced. He hated the Azmis and all they stood for. He hated that they successfully skirted the law time and again. "That's why we need to be the ones to find Jake and Jiao. Only a police contact would've known about Delgado's breakfast meeting with Jake. If Jake and Jiao are one step ahead of us, the Azmis are one step ahead of them."

The traffic slowed their unmarked cruiser. Detective Reed kept pounding away at her laptop. "You may want to sound the siren."

"Why?"

"The San Francisco police crashed Indira Cheena's apartment. They found out Jiao and Jake were there earlier today."

"Damnit, they should've waited at the sister's apartment until we got there." Detective Abbott activated the recessed LED police lights and sounded his siren. He steered left off the shoulder of the carpool lane and accelerated. "If the SFPD know about Indira then so do the Azmis. Do the police know where Jake and Jiao are going?"

"No and they don't believe Indira knows either."

Abbott weaved his way forward from road shoulder to carpool lane and back again. "Did Indira give them any information?"

"No. She told the police she wasn't involved and that Jiao and Jake were foolish to come to her."

"That doesn't ring true." He continued weaving. Lies, deception, and murder were all wrapped up in a patent, a multibillion dollar contract, and two poor souls running for their life. "We'll be near her apartment in about ten minutes with the way were moving."

"And then what?"

"Jake and Jiao are on foot. We know Hank is still in Santa Clara – so they don't have his help. They can't be that far from Indira's apartment."

"They got pretty far on foot from their Sunnyvale hideout. Jake made it to Los Altos Hills and Jiao made it to Santa Clara."

"They're resourceful, no doubt. But they're running out of options. If you were them where would you go?"

"It depends on the information they have. They've been trying to clear their name. Every move they've made was to gather information. And they don't trust us."

"Why do you say that?"

"They gave us the patent list and we didn't believe them. Jake showed up for breakfast with Delgado and was told he was going to be arrested. They handed us more investigative work than we imagined from their Sunnyvale hideout and still, the police close in on them in San Francisco. We're treating them like wanted fugitives and they're acting like wanted fugitives."

"Delgado's theory was that Jiao seduced Jake and got him to kill Amrish. That was his theory but, no matter the pressure we applied, Jake never turned on Jiao."

Detective Reed smiled. "I like that."

"You would."

"Are they a couple or were they forced into working together?"

"I've seen this happen. If they weren't a couple before, this made them one."

"Jiao and Jake have proven this is much bigger than a love triangle – even if it started out as one."

"What do you mean? You think they were complicit in Amrish's murder and then things got out of hand?"

Detective Reed paused as her partner weaved, accelerated, and stopped. She shook her head. "No. Not the way they're acting. I think there was a love triangle but this goes way beyond that."

"Then why don't they reach out to us? Since they discovered how big this thing is, they have to know we're the only ones that can help."

Both detectives' attention turned to the car display that showed an unknown number calling Detective Abbott's private line. Abbot stared at the unknown number on caller id for a moment and then hit the answer button. Sounds of footfalls and humming came over the speaker.

"What the? Hey, who's calling?"

Again they heard sounds of footfalls followed by an unintelligible panting female voice.

"Listen, this is not the number to call for a prank, you better . . ."

"Abbott, this is Jake." The voice was from someone nearly out of breath.

"Jake, where are you?"

"Golden Gate Park . . . Lalita's brother Laksh . . . drones are shooting at us."

"Jake we'll be there in minutes. When you lose this call, dial 911 and keep the line open. Do you hear me?"

There were sounds of footfalls and a groan. The line went dead.

"Drive," Detective Reed said, "or we'll have two more murders to solve."

33

Laksh looked at the drone camera images on his controller. He loved hunting. His enjoyment of the killing sport was proportional to the difficulty of the hunt. He had been on African safaris and found it thrilling at first. After a time the planned routes through the Serengeti and tour guided game drives took too much of the challenge away. He loved the killing but he also loved the sport. There was little sport in killing herded animals no matter how ferocious.

The illegal poacher hunts in India were far more exciting. The illegality and punishment if they were caught got his blood up. Many times Laksh would make and remove his kill just moments ahead of being caught. Those hunts were pure joy. The added risk made them so. The more risk, the more reward. It was only superior beings, like Laksh, who could stomach such tension. It was only superior beings, like Laksh, who could still act with calm nerves when faced with the prospect of either absolute ruin or absolute victory.

This hunt, in the middle of San Francisco's Golden Gate Park, was the best yet. This hunt had ridiculously high stakes, two intelligent fleeing people as game, and drones with underpowered weapons. This hunt was a rich experience. Laksh relished the moment. This was one of those rare times when the high adventure of lethal sport combined with the practical need to destroy the Azmis' enemies. Yes, Laksh enjoyed this hunt above all.

He planned to use the drones to wound his game and then personally finish the kills. That was the way to do it. This was personal after all. Oftentimes pursuit was an arduous, unbearably boring, undertaking. Most times his victims cowered before him. He liked the cowering as it affirmed his power but the risk was lacking. There was a nice element of risk in this hunt.

It was possible the exploding drone mini-missiles would hit one of them in the neck and finish the kill but Laksh doubted it. The missiles were underpowered for this situation. They worked on a design of a more lethal missile after the wounding attack on Jake in the Alta Mesa Cemetery but, for this hunt, he would have to get up close and personal. Laksh was glad. It made the upcoming kill all the more satisfying. And, like his illegal tiger hunts in India, there was the adrenalin inducing risk of capture. He was the only one of the Azmis who knew of the banal brutishness of distant killing. The only way to achieve fulfilment in kills was to make them like this – up close and personal.

Arjun was big on using technology to keep distance from the kills. Laksh chuckled at the thought. It wasn't about the technology. It wasn't about distance. It was about seeing the victim's fear just before the kill. Too much distance robbed the hunt of its primal enjoyment. The hunt was always about domination. It was about letting loose the beast inside. They all knew that – they all knew about the beast inside – but Laksh had lifted the beast and the joy of killing to a refined art. These two kills would be his masterpiece.

Laksh worked the controller. Both drones were linked to tandem maneuvers, avoiding trees, but staying the same distance apart. This tandem link enabled Laksh to control both drones with one controller. Two drones were perfect for flushing this game. *I need to wear them out.* He saw the two running on his screen. He imagined their fatigue, their panic, and their desperation. *The drone chase makes it all the better.*

Arjun would've balked at such a direct attack but not his sister, Lalita. All three – Arjun, Lalita, and Laksh – craved domination and all three knew to unleash the beast within to achieve it. Arjun was often satisfied with the domination achieved by summarily firing an old friend or rival. Arjun would gloat about sitting across from someone at a fine dinner, stopping the dinner, and pointing to the door for the person to exit. He reveled so much in that method of domination that he told stories, some years old, of firing friends and foes over dinner. It was all to slake the beast and extend the domination enjoyment.

Laksh and Lalita knew a different and better way. Total domination meant total destruction of your enemies. Letting his beast run loose in wild abandon was far more satisfying than Arjun's methods. It was more satisfying and it was final. Arjun would've objected to this direct attack but Lalita – Didi – was all for it.

It was time to permanently destroy their enemies. Jake and Jiao weren't just enemies, they had the audacity to oppose them. That could never be tolerated. This domination would be final. Laksh watched the two running away from his drones and the beast within howled in delight.

His drones chased the two to the edge of a cluster of tents and Laksh marveled when he saw them turn away. *They're trying to avoid collateral damage*, he thought. *What a stupid thing to do – treating homeless as if they have value.* He let the control sticks center to direct the two drones to hover in place. Laksh carefully rotated the view and saw Jake and Jiao cross Nancy Pelosi Drive. He accelerated his drones to center the missile targeting crosshairs on Jake but the two ran too fast. They got into a group of trees before he could fire.

Laksh smiled. His game had more stamina that he would have guessed. He increased the altitude of his armed drones and moved them over the treetops. His game couldn't hide in Golden Gate Park since there were as many open spaces as wooded area. He cruised his drones over the trees, swung them around to face the exit from the woods and waited. He stared at the irregular line of trees for a few moments and realized they changed direction.

He flicked the sensor control and enabled infrared view. This view served as a locater but didn't have the precision necessary to fire his missiles. He swung the drones from side to side and noticed the heat signature of the two in the top left corner of his display. Jake Hawes and Jiao Liu were worthy opponents. They didn't run straight through the trees but were following the cover parallel to Nancy Pelosi Drive. He zoomed his drones toward them.

Laksh followed the heat signatures above the tree cover until he was directly above them and then switched back to optical sensors. The two broke into the open as they got the end of Nancy Pelosi Drive and crossed Martin Luther King Jr. Drive. This was the shot Laksh was looking for. He led the Jake and Jiao with his targeting crosshairs and fired two missiles.

The moment he fired he knew he'd missed. Three steps onto Martin Luther King Jr. Drive the couple jerked hard left and his two missiles crashed into the road. The mini-missile impacts looked like tiny bright puffs on his display. Across Martin Luther King Jr. Drive, Jake and Jiao got into tree cover again. Laksh cursed himself. *I must remember this isn't ordinary game. These are skilled adversaries and I keep underestimating them.*

He flicked the sensor back to infrared and increased his drones' altitude. *The trick*, he thought, *is to be unpredictable. It was obvious to them that I would fire when they broke into the clear.* He kept his drones over and behind Jake and Jiao as they ran, satisfied that the drones were driving them onward. No matter how clever these human animals were, this chase had to be exhausting.

Laksh moved his drones to even higher altitude. As long as the hum was enough to keep them moving, it would only be a matter of time. He watched the heat signatures as Jake and Jiao ran west. Laksh resisted targeting them when they crossed narrow footpaths. He kept them in sight and he kept them moving.

Jake and Jiao were running parallel to Martin Luther King Jr. Drive and as they ran Laksh followed with his drones. Laksh saw something he didn't think his prey would. The drive curved down nearly next to Lincoln Way. Once they got to the end of the Martin Luther King Jr. Drive curve they would be in the open no matter which way they turned.

Laksh flicked his sensor to optical and focused his targeting crosshairs on the opening before Crossover Drive. He spaced his aim to allow both drones to fire with a spread. In a satisfying view, Jake and Jiao broke into the open and began to sprint across Crossover Drive. He saw them juke right. *Not this time.* He led them perfectly with a good target crosshair spread. He squeezed the fire button and saw one of his missiles hit its target. *Patience pays off.* He smiled and his beast within whooped.

34

Jiao staggered under the jolt of pain and force of the blow. She screamed and it was only her momentum that kept her moving across the road. As she stumbled Jake caught her arm and hustled her into tree cover. The pain was like nothing she'd ever felt. It was a combination of a burning center and expanding sharp pinpricks, all throbbing and swamping her consciousness.

Jake said something and she clutched onto him with all her strength. The act of hanging onto Jake was all her mind could muster. The pain in her lower back was all consuming. She gasped and staggered. She felt Jake's arm across her back and under her legs at the knees. Through the haze of pain she felt Jake carry her. That gave Jiao comfort. Her consciousness dulled.

She fought against the haze. There were important things to do. Jiao knew that but she couldn't sort her thoughts. Things flashed in her mind's eye. Amrish, a philosopher's stone patent – a storage device, Arjun, ACES Corporation, Indira, Laksh . . . and Jake. Yes, that was important. Jake was important. "Jake . . ."

"Don't try to talk. I hear a siren. I'll get you help."

Jake's voice reassured her. He was breathing hard from their start-stop running but his voice exuded control. *Yes*, Jiao thought. *I can trust this voice. I can trust this man.* There were things she needed to tell him. There were too many unsaid important things. Why was it always that way? Why was she always quiet until it was too late?

She felt jolts of pain with every one of Jake's strides. There was something urgent she hadn't done. Jiao felt her heart flutter. There was a thing they still had to do and she had to tell him. Her lungs seemed shallow and she gasped breaths in quick pants. Her mind struggled to work. They had something important to do and she had to tell Jake. What was it? Faintness threatened to overtake her.

"The drones are staying high. I think that was their last shot."

That comment struck Jiao as nonsensical. What was it she needed to tell him? She was doing something that focused all her energy and they were running, running with the whine of drones overhead. She had run in a sprint to keep up with Jake, fearful that she would slow him down and they'd be overtaken.

Jiao had never run as fast and as long as she did across Golden Gate Park before being struck, before being shot by that damnable drone. She struggled to understand. Was it the drone shot or the run that induced this shock? She was in a state of shock. Of that, she had no doubt. Knowing that didn't enable her to overcome her lightheaded pulse-racing thought-quenching panting.

Shock didn't matter. She lost something. There was something that she had and now she lost it. There was something important to do that couldn't be done now. There was something she had to say. She remembered. "Computer . . . I dropped computer."

"Can't be helped. We need to get you an ambulance."

Again, Jake's comment was nonsensical. What good would an ambulance do with drones overhead and enemies all around? Jiao lifted her head off of Jake's shoulder and wooziness overtook her. She lay her head back and groaned. There was nothing she could do but trust Jake. He knew of the computer. He knew of the importance of the information. And she could trust him.

Jiao clung to that single thought over the pain and doubts. She could trust Jake. She loved him and would put all in his hands. She loved him. She loved the man with an awkward sense of humor, a good head, and a stout heart. She felt his grip tighten on her. She relished the feel of his strong arms carrying her through these trees away from their enemies. A warmth flushed her once pale cheeks, from emotion or fever – she didn't know.

She felt Jake stop and pant. His breaths were solid reassurance of life and love. He twisted around. "Oh … don't." Jiao's voice came out as a low exhale. What were the important things? Her life had compressed to a thread of consciousness in the midst of a rush of pain. She waded through her jumbled thoughts to find the pearl.

Their flight from the moment they left her townhouse was one of peril and promise. For all the threats and fears, Jake never wavered. That was the most important thing she clung to. And there was more. There was a world changing patent, out in public for decades that finally bore fruit. There was a mixed up married boss who loved her and died trying to protect her. There were murders done for nothing more than power. There was a sister who yearned to avenge her brother's death but she feared for her life. Through it all, there was Jake.

The time with Jake in the Residence Inn and their hideout was the adventure of her lifetime. They acted as heroes in a dull grey world dominated by corrupt power brokers like the Azmis. She had never known such action was possible.

She had never felt such a rush of excitement. She had never felt such tender love and such cold fear. She had never felt such a bolt of pain. Their enemies were like nothing she'd ever faced. They weren't just trying to outsmart them, their enemies were trying to kill them. Perhaps they would be destroyed but, surrounded by death and enemies, they fought on, inadequate as those efforts proved to be.

Jake and his military friends would often use words like noble goal and character and duty. Jiao respected the idea of those values as much as Jake. But she saw Jake's respect for those values had turned into raw sentiment. She once viewed that sentiment as naive. In the harsh world where over six and a half million in Hong Kong get handed over from one power to the next without a say, what good was sentiment of noble values? What good was character?

But Jake taught her. He taught her these values were not naïve. The values Jake espoused were the living breathing pulses of the upward thrust of humanity. These values moved the world more than any power, corrupt or not. Jake taught her that character was the motive force more powerful even than efficient electricity storage. Jake taught her by acting and living and risking all.

Jiao once thought pure love was an equally naïve sentiment. She once thought that love was equal measures of practicality and opportunity. Never, till this moment, did she view love as a joint quest in the pursuit of the prize that can only be gained by a partnership acting on great values.

She felt Jake pick up the pace for several steps and stop. How much time was passing? The whine of the drones increased to a high pitch. That whine told her time was passing in slow minutes and not hours. She knew the limits of drone batteries that powered that whine. The drone shot caused her shock but she was coming out of it.

"Jake, where are you going?" Her voice came out with a force that surprised her.

Jiao felt him stop. She felt his lips on hers and wrapped her arm around him. She slid her hand to the back of his neck and drank in the frantic passion. The pain and desperation that swamped her consciousness now mixed with love. She clung to the love. She clung to Jake and, if this were her last moments, she wanted them to be filled with love.

"I'm going to find help." Jake's voice was edged with determination. "Detective Abbott's coming. I have the phone on. We'll be found."

"I love you." Jiao only had that one sentence to say.

"Jiao . . . I love you too and I'm going to get you help."

She felt his lips on hers again and she knew this was the end. Her wooziness returned and she heaved a deep sigh. "Thank you Jake . . ."

35

Jake looked through the trees to the road. Jiao was limp in his arms. The sound of the drones was a constant unwanted companion. Time had slowed to a crawl. His mind flashed to the thought that these may be his last moments. There was no doubt they faced an enemy intending to kill them.

He ran, carrying Jiao, in the tree cover of Golden Gate Park parallel to Lincoln Way. He willed the siren and help to come. He had the burner phone in his pocket still on the 911 call. Help would come but would it be in time? He doubted it. Everything had unraveled in his life – his first marriage, his job, his friendship with Amrish, his plan to stop Arjun and the Azmis – all unwound into this desperate impossible situation.

He felt Jiao stir. This woman – this amazing brilliant woman – was all he had. His life was now in middle age, he couldn't deny that. And incredible as it was, in his middle age, he found love. Was that right? Jake thought so. He hoped it was right. This woman with her brilliance, toughness, and tenderness redefined love for him.

Jake had first flirted with Jiao as type of sport. Jiao conceded to accept his attention. He knew she viewed their first attachment as a practical thing offering companionship and physical pleasure. They used each other for their own ends. He knew it and accepted it. He didn't think it was more than a practical arrangement until he lost her. When Jiao went to Amrish and bonded with him, Jake was lost.

Jake saw the situation with clear eyes. He was Jiao's convenient escort to be discarded the moment someone smarter came along. And Amrish, like Jiao and most others in the Silicon Valley, was smarter. That was the thing. All of Jake's bravado, shining character, and yearned for heroics were rejected as out of place. He was the proverbial square peg in a round hole that would never fit into Silicon Valley. He would never fit into someone like Doctor Jiao Liu's life.

His arms throbbed with fatigue and his lungs burned. *Move, I have to keep moving.* He went from tree to tree. The woman in his arms surprised him the last few days. She used her vaunted laser focus in partnership with him. They struggled side by side to find answers and the results of that struggle were Jake's greatest accomplishment. That she viewed him as a partner, that she gave him physical tenderness, that she trusted him once again; all that made Jake love her like he never thought possible.

But that love and all it meant to him would be for nothing if Laksh won. All that Jiao meant to him would be for nothing if the Azmis won. If his character meant anything at all then this challenge, in the middle age of his life, was the truest test. Whatever was left of effort in his heart and soul he threw into this struggle.

He kept moving. He forced the drones to maneuver and descend to keep tracking him. He stayed in the trees moving from one to another in a slow steady pace. He had to trade movement for time. Jiao depended on him. That Jiao was shot by the devil Laksh required vengeance. Laksh hurt this dazzling woman who showed Jake love was possible. Jake bubbled in rage and pushed it down. *Think and move. Think and move.*

Jake always knew he had the capacity for heroics. Or at least he had the capacity for the attempt of heroics. The reach for something greater, the confrontation with adversity, the test of character; these were his dreams, once forgotten. The murder that resulted in teaming with Jiao first as companions and then as lovers, changed everything. The quest they were on was noble and against the worst that humanity could throw at them.

That Jiao embraced the quest and embraced Jake filled him with wonder. They did things beyond what even he imagined in his dreams of the heroic. They were on the edge of something truly great. But all his heroics would mean nothing without Jiao. She was hurt and there was an evil hunter nearly upon them.

He slowed and realized the drones weren't tracking him as close as they once were. He realized they were doing something worse. He remembered driving deer when hunting in West Virginia. It was the same thing in this urban area. Jake was slowed by his need to carry Jiao and was in a confined area. The drones were driving him into a kill zone. Laksh was using the drones not just to track his movement but to direct it – and to exhaust him in the process.

There had to be a way to turn this fight. He needed help. He willed with all his might that help arrive so he could get Jiao to safety. Jake knew Detective Abbott must be close. He looked left and saw a dark car with flashing red LED lights and heard a pulsing siren. He turned left and, in five quick steps, broke into the clear on Lincoln Way.

The sirens blared and the police car accelerated. It came to a screeching stop next to them. Detective Abbott and a blonde woman came out of the car. They ran up to Jake. "Help her!" Jake said. "Laksh shot her."

Detective Abbott helped Jake lower Jiao to the curb. Jake saw the blonde woman draw her weapon and point it toward the park. The drone whine rose and then dimmed. Jake saw the two drones climb to such height they were dots in the sky.

"Bonnie, get the first aid kit from the car and call an ambulance," Detective Abbott said.

Jiao heard Detective Abbott and smiled. She was safe. There was no need to fear. The man in the pink blazer, Laksh, couldn't hurt them now. Footsteps came up behind her and Abbot rolled her toward him. "Cut her blouse off. She has shrapnel in her lower back."

Shrapnel? These are really metal blades. She felt slathering pain that made her groan as the fabric was pulled away from her wound. *I need to pull myself together. Was it the shock or the wound that makes me woozy?* No matter. She lifted her head and opened her eyes. Detective Abbott stared at her with a concerned apologetic gaze. "Did you . . . get our stuff in Sunnyvale?" Her voice was a breathy whisper.

"We got it," Detective Abbott said. "You two did some great investigative work. Now, stay still for a moment. Detective Reed is going to put some antibiotic salve on that wound."

She felt the cool salve being spread on her back. "Nice, do you have water?"

"We'll get you some." Abbott extended a tall cup. "Do you want coffee?"

Jiao took the cup and drank a long sip of coffee. The caffeine hit her system like bolt. She sat up.

"Easy," Detective Reed said behind her. "I need to tape this bandage in place. You'll have to go to the hospital to get the shrapnel removed."

Jiao pushed her mental transmit button and her words spilled out in a stream. "Amrish discovered a public domain superconductor storage patent and realized it would enable everyone to store power in trough periods for use in peak times. This patent threatened Arjun and Lalita's plans to lock up California renewable energy contracts and they sent their henchman Laksh, who wears a pink blazer, to kill us. He's been following us with his drones and that's how I got shot."

"Take it easy Doctor Liu," Detective Abbott said. "We know most of what you just said."

Detective Reed stepped away and returned with a water bottle. She extended it to Jiao. "You guys gave us quite a scare."

"That's what I need." Jiao took the water, unscrewed the cap, and drank half the bottle down in one long gulp. "Oh, I'm going to be okay."

"Did you find any more evidence here in San Francisco?" Detective Abbott asked.

"We did." She looked around. "I lost the Chromebook and the USB drive when running from the drone but Jake has a drive." She looked left and right. "Where's Jake?"

36

The drones hovered overhead as Jake ran. He took the opportunity to escape when Detective Abbott and Detective Reed were hunched over Jiao. He ran straight into Golden Gate Park. He didn't stop when he crossed Martin Luther King Jr. Drive or, moments later, when he crossed Middle Drive. He crossed a footpath and a running track and ran into an open field. He ran straight into the middle of the Golden Gate Park Polo Field. He looked up at the descending drones.

The drones lowered to a point across from Jake. He confirmed that they had changed from attack to tracking. He saw empty missile pods below each. Jake's rage bubbled and boiled. He pointed straight at the drone cameras as they came to eye level. He tapped his chest. "You and me, no one else!" He pointed to the woods adjacent the polo field. He ran east across the polo field, over a footpath, and into the woods.

This was a rash and reckless move. There was evidence in the USB drive in his pocket as well as what Jake and Jiao provided by their evening reconnaissance activities. Their enemies were strong. Both he and Jiao had been wounded and Jake knew they would be killed if their enemies were given the chance. It was folly in all ways – except for one thing.

Jake knew something his adversary didn't. He knew of his demon. Jake knew that he, like Hank and everyone else for that matter, had a dark demon. Most suppress or ignore their darkness. Most live their lives never knowing about the terror and icy enjoyment the demon provides. Discovering the demon comes first, then comes the ability to use it. And Jake knew how to use his dark demon. His knowledge was hard won.

In desert sands with death all around Jake discovered his darkness. Horror and denial afterwards didn't change that discovery. He'd talked at length with Hank and realized his demon was part of his humanity. It was part of everyone's humanity. It was the dark force, Freud's Id, a snarling monster that drove instinctual aggressive action. It was the part of humanity that everyone put in a cage and denied until most forgot it existed. Jake jogged east deeper into the woods.

But the demon did exist. Denying it wasn't helping humanity. Jake acknowledged his dark force and kept it caged. That most never find out about their personal demon didn't change that all have one. Knowing that gave Jake a sense of the evil he faced. It was the evil ones, weaned on use of force to solve problems, who wielded demonic power. There was a line in the actions of humanity that, once crossed, couldn't be reversed. That's why their enemy was so formidable. The evil ones, like Laksh, become their demon.

Jake knew that Laksh was consumed by the unleashed strength of his dark force. It was a heady transcendent darkness. The dark force, the demon, was hidden in some souls. In others, like Jake or Hank, the dark force manifested itself in times of great peril and scarred the soul. In the evil, the dark force overtook the soul. That was the source of their power and their ability to induce fear. Laksh had become his demon, he had become a remnant of humanity.

Whether stirred by a quest for domination or in response to a perceived slight, Jake knew Laksh couldn't resist his challenge. Laksh's instinctual reaction would be as swift as it was certain. Jake threatened him and his family. There was no bringing that red hate down. Jake knew that Laksh now used his fury as fuel in this fight. Jake figured Laksh's hate was hot. He doubted Laksh had any idea how cool rage worked.

Jake would control and use his dark force. He could use his personal demon in a slow burn of cool rage. He crossed John F. Kennedy Drive and kept jogging into another wooded area going due east. What Laksh couldn't know was that Jake had a demon of equal power to his own. What Laksh couldn't know was that Jake had just let his demon out of its cage.

It was the first time since the sands of Iraq that Jake had let his dark force loose. He had talked about his demon with fellow 13th Infantry Division veteran Hank Rudzinski but neither had ever let their demon run free – until now. Until Laksh shot Jiao from the coward's perch of a drone missile.

No retribution save Laksh's utter destruction would suffice. Jake's instinctual drive for hate filled retribution and total destruction moved him forward. Laksh was coming after Jake as if he were a beaten exhausted animal. Laksh wouldn't know he was facing a combat veteran who just uncaged his killing demon. And that, and only that, was Jake's advantage. Jake relished in the invigoration from his murderous rage.

Jake crossed Transverse Drive and ran onto the wide Crossover Drive. He stopped and mimed shooting an overhead drone with his finger. He ran further east into the woods. *I'm far enough away that Detective Abbott won't find me for a while. We have the setting for our showdown.* A showdown is what Jake wanted. Nothing less would do.

His plan was to run far enough toward Laksh to force a one on one confrontation. The showdown was the red meat his dark force demanded. Confrontation was the essence of the aggressive instinct. It was as old as humanity itself, a barbarism resulting in wars, terrorism, and murder.

Confrontation was also the essence of courage as a base of character, of the noble, of the heroic. Jake knew that was why he never tired of watching the movie, *Rocky*. In the end, every great thing is done by winning a confrontation, every great thing involves winning a fight. The longer the odds, the better.

Jake knew the odds in this fight, even with his demon uncaged, didn't favor him. But the attack on Jiao demanded nothing less. Any fear of failure had to be squelched, otherwise all was lost. Thus Jake's dark force, his unholy demon, did its work. He had courage borne of cool rage.

He was using his unholy demon in a holy confrontation. Everything that meant anything to Jake was opposed by the Azmis. This evil family meant to expand their corruption into an unstoppable force. They wanted to take, by graft and force, this great state's fortune and future. If they succeeded now, there was no telling how far and wide their evil influence would spread. And they stopped at nothing. There was no obstacle, even if that obstacle was the brilliant woman Jake loved, the Azmis wouldn't crush underfoot to achieve their ends.

That evil resolve, backed by Laksh's force, could only be defeated by equal fortitude, by sheer grit that right must prevail. Jake would meet this test. His fight with Laksh was everything Jake dreamed. The stakes were nothing less than life and death, love and hate, good and evil. To be worthy of Jiao's love, there was only one path. There was no retreat and no hesitation.

His adrenalin surged through his veins and gave him heightened alertness. The two drones moved east in front of him and descended out of sight. He heard the rotors wind down. This was it. The drones landed and Laksh was coming. This was the place for the showdown.

He noted that to his left, on Park Presidio Boulevard, a dark van slowed. The drones landed out of sight in front of him. *There must be a clearing. That's where Laksh would want it to happen – in a clearing against an unarmed man.* Jake had other ideas. He paused at a drainage culvert hidden from view of the van and searched. He smiled when he saw a baseball sized rock. He picked up the perfect weapon. Now, he needed cover. Jake moved east and his demon growled with pleasure.

37

Detective Abbott cursed. How could they have let Jake disappear? He was next to Jiao one moment and gone the next. All of their carefully planned interrogation and evidence hung in the balance. If Jake got himself killed and Laksh disappeared, there'd be no end to court battles.

He stared with dismay into the wooded area of the Golden Gate Park. Detective Abbott saw no way for Jake to survive a confrontation with a trained killer. No matter how skilled and resourceful, Jake was outgunned and outmanned. *Why? Why would he go after Laksh alone and unarmed?*

"How could you let him go?" Jiao was in a lather. "You have to find him."

Detective Abbott turned to Jiao. "Was Jake armed? Did he have a gun?"

"No. You need to find him."

That was the task, Abbott realized. But procedure mandated he wait for backup. There was no provision for the detective to go in pursuit single-handed in an area that was out of his jurisdiction. *Why would Jake go in there unarmed?* The detective couldn't make sense of it. Was there someplace safe in the park Jake would go? He turned again to Jiao. "Where would he go?"

"He went after Laksh." Jiao, nearly unconscious moments ago, rose to her feet. She looked east into the wooded area Jake carried her through. "You must find him."

"Doctor Liu," Detective Reed said as she clasped Jiao's arm. "Your ambulance will be here in minutes."

"You must find Jake. He's gone after Laksh."

Detective Abbott turned toward her. In all his years of police work, he had never seen anything like this. He had never seen anyone do what Jake was doing now. It was obvious that Jiao was in love with this man. Why wouldn't Jake stay with her? Why would Jake go to his certain death? Laksh was a killer, a thug. He wasn't Arjun Azmi. "Why would Jake go after Laksh?"

"Laksh is the key to everything. He is the key to pinning all this – the button murders, the patent, framing us – everything on the Azmis."

That was new news. And it made twisted sense. As the evidence they recovered from the vacant office building showed, the Azmis were into everything including heroin drug smuggling. The Azmis were part of the opiate epidemic burning out the soul of America's vulnerable. When drugs were involved, lethal muscle was always needed. It seemed that lethal muscle was Lalita's brother, Laksh.

The murder case that started as a simple open and shut love triangle had expanded beyond comprehension. Laksh was the Azmi muscle who killed Amrish. Laksh was the one who got his partner, Detective Delgado, killed. Laksh was worth going after. And he was in the park at this moment.

The detective stared east into the woods and again, felt admiration for what Jake was attempting. He had seen it time and again. The disgust with the slow progress of the authorities resulted in lack of confidence. The disgust with cronyism and corruption led people to dismiss the badged authority.

That lack of trust in authority was why individuals insisted on owning guns to protect themselves. That was why finding witnesses to crimes was so difficult. That was why cooperation with police was at an all-time low. *I need to retire*, Detective Abbot thought. *When someone like Jake feels he's got to do this alone, we've lost all trust.*

Regardless of the reason, what Jake was attempting was folly. An unarmed man going against a trained killer packing a personal arsenal was certain to fail. "Jake is in over his head. He should let the professionals handle it."

"You professionals never believed us."

There it was. There couldn't be a plainer statement of the lack of trust. Their car radio came to life with San Francisco police dispatch hailing them. Detective Bonnie Reed turned toward the car. The call came again.

"I got it," Detective Abbott said. The detective reached in the open window and pulled the radio microphone to his mouth. "This is Abbott."

"We're still recording a 911 call on an open line we believe is from Jake Hawes. If you've located him, we'll drop that line."

"No, don't. Jake is in the Golden Gate Park and there are criminals here with armed drones. We know an active shooter is in the park as well. Keep that line open and keep recording."

"Okay Abbot. We've been misinformed and have already redirected your backup to a higher priority scene."

Detective Abbott's icy dismay increased. He forced himself to speak in a calm tone. "There are armed drones and active shooters at this location. Please send back up here immediately." He looked at Detective Reed who stood with wide eyes at the exchange as she propped Jiao in a standing position.

"You have to get to Jake," Jiao said. She was fully alert after the coffee, water, and rest. She grabbed Detective Abbott's arm and fixed him with a desperate pleading gaze. "There's no time."

"We confirm continuing need for backup at Golden Gate Park." The dispatcher's voice was deadpan. "Stabilize the situation and do not enter the park. We expect units to arrive at your location in ten to fifteen minutes."

"Do you understand me?" Detective Abbott felt helpless under Jiao's gaze and the asinine directions from dispatch. "There are active shooters in the park."

"We'll see if we can expedite backup." The receive call light blinked off.

"Are you kidding me?" Detective Abbott said aloud. He dropped the microphone on the car seat.

"Detective Abbott please listen," Jiao said. "Jake is going after the man who killed Amrish. He's going after the man who killed your partner, Detective Delgado. You need to help him."

"No one told him to do that. I ought to arrest the both of you."

"For what? For getting shot by the guy you won't go after?"

"Doctor Liu, you are way out of line . . ."

A loud reverberating bang of a gunshot came from the park. The gunshot sound echoed. That gunshot echo was a rebuke of the detective's inaction and it crystallized his duty. Detective Abbott turned from Jiao to Detective Reed. "Stay with her. I'm going after him."

"We're supposed to wait for backup."

Detective Abbott was done waiting. The gunshot sound galvanized him into action. He unholstered his sidearm, chambered a round, and entered the Golden Gate Park from Lincoln Way.

38

aksh watched the homeless man fall in front of him, a spout of blood arcing from his chest. *Why would such a vermin get in front of me?* The sound still reverberated and he cursed his haste. *I should've put on my silencer, this will shorten the time I have to take care of Jake Hawes.* The man gurgled and tried to say something. *That death is on you Jake.*

He took another glance at the dying man. A woman and two children ran up. The woman wailed and a stream of Spanish followed Laksh as he moved into the sparse woods away from the tent cluster. He would've preferred a silencer but no matter.

The Spanish intonations behind him rose to a crescendo. Laksh's ire rose as he distanced himself from the victim. If that victim understood rules of force and power, he'd still be alive. Hell, if that victim's ancestors understood the rules of force the states of California, Arizona, New Mexico, Colorado, and Texas would still be part of Mexico.

Laksh knew enough history to take a long view. The Spanish took this land from the natives through brute force. The Spanish had guns and the natives didn't. The resulting Mexican nation achieved their independence through that same type of brute force. Then the gringos came and took the land with a violence and determination that stunned the Mexicans. The need for the rulers, whomever they were, to use increased violence was due to one key tenet. If you want to rule, you kill your enemies.

Now that the gringos were a spent power, it was time for those like the Azmis to assume supremacy. It was their time to rule. And Laksh was the Azmis soldier to apply the needed force. This very moment, he was doing exactly what the rulers before him had done. He was going to kill their enemy. If there was collateral damage like the homeless man behind him, so be it.

The wails of grief faded as he moved toward Jake. He still had time but he had to hustle. The wails and destruction he left behind didn't matter. The world was full of worthless sheep like the meddling man he just ended. That happened to all timid people who forgot how the world worked. Those timid people became sheep in a world controlled by others.

Laksh was not from a family of sheep. He and his sister Lalita allied themselves with the rising power in both California and India – Arjun Azmi. The Azmis' reach was broad and deep. It would soon include a fifty-year multi-billion dollar contract and elected officials in both countries. The Azmis would rule because they were unflinching when it came time to use lethal force.

The Azmis would rule because they had Laksh and he was bold in pursuing their enemies. The cliché was true. The world belongs to the bold. Laksh was not only bold, he moved with decisiveness while others dithered. No one ever accused him of hesitation.

Laksh ran, brandishing his Glock 9mm pistol, deeper into the Golden Gate Park making a beeline for his drones, making a beeline for Jake. There was a lot to take care of. After killing Jake, he and his accomplice, Chuck, had to secure the drones and make their getaway. Laksh snorted thinking of the drones. The drones needed an upgrade.

He needed to fit the drones with lethal missiles. Had that been done earlier, this problem would already be solved. A weapon as versatile as an armed drone was only effective if it destroyed rather than wounded their enemy. Laksh slowed and took careful steps when seeing an opening in front of him.

He also had to refresh his police contacts. The Azmi contacts had managed to delay the arrival of more units at Golden Gate Park but, as the police scanner indicated, the delay was only for ten minutes. Ten minutes was enough to do this job but it was nothing like he'd arranged in a similar hunt in East Palo Alto.

Laksh stopped behind the Conservatory of Flowers and tried to get his bearings. There were too damn many tents around. He pulled his encrypted two way radio off his hip and pushed the transmit button. "Chuck, hit your horn so I know where to go."

"I'm staring at your man now," Chuck's voice came over the radio. "Get here and get this done."

Two dull horn honks oriented Laksh. He ran, slowed at John F. Kennedy Drive to await a passing car, and sprinted across the road and into the woods. This was going to be a lot closer than he wanted but there was no turning back. Killing Jake would stop one big source of damning information. That and their contacts might be enough to finish the energy contracts and secure themselves for the next fifty years.

Then again, killing Jake might not be enough. Once you started down the killing people path, you had to be thorough. Otherwise your enemies could regroup. Leaving angry allies of the dead behind wasn't wise. The delayed killing of Amrish showed as much. You had to be thorough and it had to be final. Machiavelli was right. Destruction of your enemies and the fear it engendered were the base of sustained power. *Jake won't be enough*, he thought. *First I get Jake, then we regroup and get Jiao Liu.*

He broke out of a lightly wooded area onto Music Concourse Drive. *Damn!* He hit his radio. "Chuck, one more time."

The horn honked again. "Go north toward Fulton Street. Your man is coming toward you going east."

What kind of idiot was Jake to come after him? It made no sense. *He must be exhausted and leading me away from his lover.* That was the only explanation. Jake was sacrificing himself. What a ridiculous pointless gesture. Laksh would take Jake's sacrifice but he hated the idea. Sacrifice was the opposite of a dominating power play. Sacrifices only drove a group forward for a time . . . until they were all dead.

Laksh ran right and crossed John F. Kennedy Drive again. He was taken aback by the presence of the large de Young Museum in front of him. His initial thought was that the Golden Gate Park was perfect for the conclusion of his hunt. The clusters of tents, the homeless man who accosted him, and all these buildings were unexpected difficulties. But there was an idiot he must kill and, in running toward him, Jake was making it easier.

Laksh stopped when he saw Fulton Street and turned left, crossed 10th Avenue, and entered a thickly wooded area. He slowed. This area may be behind the museum but it afforded him good cover and Chuck was right there. He could finish Jake, pop out onto Fulton Street, and make his escape. *Okay lover boy, come sacrifice yourself.*

He slowed his breathing. He would upgrade his drones but now, he was thankful the drones didn't have lethal missiles. This hunt was personal. Laksh would relish this kill.

Years from now, when the Azmis were supreme across the land and across the world, Laksh would tell stories of this moment. He would tell the story of how this was the moment where he killed the last enemy that could stop them. This was the moment the Azmis' empire was secured.

"This way asshole – gaandu!" Jake's taunt hit him like a slap across his face.

Laksh's wrath bubbled into consuming fury. He leveled his pistol and slunk toward the voice.

39

Jake saw Laksh and sensed his arrogance. The moment he saw him, he realized how right he was to abandon Jiao and force this confrontation. He saw in Laksh a man who moved above the law and beyond all sense of justice.

He had heard the shot and knew that a homeless person, like the one who saved him at the Interstate 85 underpass, got in Laksh's way. Jake watched his foe and saw a man who killed at will. He saw a man who enabled evil to triumph. He saw the lethal muscle of the Azmi clan and knew the only way to stop them was to stop Laksh.

Jake's demon, a sense more than a voice, urged caution. There was a detail that needed solved. Laksh had a pistol and knew how to use it. Jake had nothing but his wits and a rock. As good as that may be, he still needed surprise. He had to close the distance so his demon could howl. *To clear our names, to do the right thing but, most of all, for Jiao . . . I'm going to kill you.*

His hatred expanded and he welcomed the darkness. It was important to define the task. This was kill or be killed. Only one was walking out of this cluster of trees alive. He let the hate spread and warm him. Jake knew this hate would scar his soul but he also knew it was the only weapon that gave him a chance. He trembled in breathless anticipation.

Laksh moved through the woods with crackling sounds at each step. He swung his pistol from side to side and Jake noticed that Laksh was in a distracted rage. That was the wrong manner for combat. Laksh's movements were hurried. He was in a rush to get this over with. Laksh knew the police would be here in minutes.

It wouldn't do for the police to come before their confrontation. The only way to win this fight was to destroy his enemy. Stalling wasn't the plan. Jake used his controlled rage to keep his focus and keep calm.

He moved with noiseless light steps, staying in a crouch and in deep shadow. He looked at the sharp edged baseball sized piece of granite in his hand. This was his only weapon and he would have only one shot. His demon would only have one chance to howl.

Laksh said something and pulled a radio from his hip. Jake pushed down a surge of fury at seeing Laksh's dismissive attitude. That attitude gave him an advantage if he could use it. Jake moved to attack Laksh from the side, from an unexpected direction. A twig cracked underfoot on one of his sidesteps. Laksh lowered the radio, clipped it to his belt, and leveled his pistol on a line to the left of Jake.

Laksh was in a small opening. "Jake, let's get this over with you worthless piece of shit."

Oh we will Laksh, of that you may be sure. Jake circled right and stepped to the last tree offering concealment. Once he was in the clearing, all would be over in a blink. Jake was a coiled spring, his thoughts awash in anticipation. He waited as Laksh looked his direction. Jake could feel the steady beats of his heart. This moment of pause was an eternity. Laksh turned his gaze away and Jake made his move.

Jake stepped around the tree. *I get only one shot.* He struck his old high school pitcher's throwing pose, told his demon to throw true, and launched the rock in a perfect arc toward Laksh. "Here asshole."

The moment the rock left his hand Jake dove right. The throw felt strong and true. Laksh swiveled toward him and fired. Jake felt a bolt of pain punch his left side. He kept his head up as he hit the ground and saw the rock strike Laksh just above the bridge of his nose.

Perfect throw. The rock strike induced a burst of elation. His enemy was wounded. *Now, move!* Jake scrambled to his feet through the haze of pain. Laksh staggered backward a step, blood streaming from his nose. He squeezed off another shot in Jake's general direction. But Jake was up and running in a pounding bull rush toward Laksh and the shot went wide. Step, step, launch.

Jake caught Laksh's forearm and swung the pistol away as he drove his the top of his head into Laksh's chin. The force of the impact carried Laksh off his feet and backward. Laksh squeezed off one more shot to the side before the sudden ground impact loosened his grip on the pistol. Jake lifted his head and saw the pistol pinwheel away. His killing demon was in a lather.

Jake leaned back and cocked his fist. Time had slowed and in the milliseconds where his muscles tensed his hate waxed. Jake saw in Laksh's pompous face all that was evil, all that had to be destroyed. His demon consumed him and Jake became the destroyer himself, full of righteous venom. His muscles uncoiled, unleashing his fist like a shot from a cannon. Jake launched his punch with all his weight, strength, and near blind fury into the side of Laksh's face. The impact was so hard he could feel bones crack.

Laksh wailed in agony. The sound filled Jake with ecstasy. Laksh's wail was confirmation that Jake had won. It was confirmation of the destruction of his foe. For the first time since Desert Storm, his killing demon's thirst was slaked.

Jake swiveled back feeling pure joy at his foe's destruction. His eyes were wide, drool dripped from his mouth. His mixed hate and joy of this total domination was a drug that turned Jake into an animal. He growled open mouthed and teeth bearing as he swung his fist into Laksh's temple. He felt a dull crack and the satisfying limpness of his attacker.

Jake slowly swiveled back, his eyes murderous, drool still dripping from his mouth. He eyed Laksh's Adam's apple and knew this would be the killing blow. Only death would suffice. The kill or be killed mantra had been reduced to this moment. It was time to kill.

A man gripped him from behind. "Jake, stop!" Jake was pulled off Laksh and the voice resolved to clarity. "Doctor Liu is okay. You got him. We have the evidence. We know it was the Azmis."

Jake recognized the voice was that of Detective Abbott. His demon, poised to kill, wrestled against his reason. Jake's demon howled that his enemy was prone below him. He used a sliver of reason to cling to one thing opposing his unleashed hate. He clung to that thought against his bubbling fury.

He gasped and hung onto that bright thread against the darkness for all he was worth. Jake panted and panted, forcing himself to calm. The bright thread expanded and the only force able to overcome his hate surfaced in his psyche. He turned to the detective. "Jiao?"

"She's okay."

Jake exhaled and, only then, got his dark demon back in its cage. He felt a rush of lightheadedness and lost consciousness.

40

Jake opened his eyes and saw Hank Rudzinski staring at him. He looked around and realized he was in a hospital room.

"13th Infantry Division Desert Storm veteran and U.S. Army Ranger highly trained in combat." Hank shook his head. "The best you could come up with was going after the bad guy with a rock in your hand?" He smiled.

"Hank, whew . . . that was urban combat. Hand to hand combat."

"I figured. You hit Laksh so hard you broke your hand in five places." Hank stared at his friend.

"What?"

"Did you get your demon back in its cage?"

Jake turned away from Hank and stared at the ceiling. He frowned. "I think so. I hope I did."

"Yeah, you don't want him running loose."

"You got that right." Jake smiled at his friend. "At least I didn't name my demon like you did yours."

"I'm glad you made it Jake."

Jake started. "Jiao?"

"She's right here. I'll leave you two alone."

Jake turned to the side opposite Hank and saw Jiao in a wheelchair with a connected intravenous drip. "Hey love, are you okay?"

Jiao blushed and wheeled next to him. She looked past Jake. "Thank you Hank. You are a true friend."

"I'll see you guys later." Hank left the room.

Jiao turned to Jake. Her pupils dilated into a loving gaze. "I'm fine Jake." Her cheeks were rosy and a warm smile creased her lips. "You really did it."

Jake lifted his hand and noticed it was in a bulky cast. "Look at that."

Jiao chuckled. "You broke Laksh's jaw in six places, knocked out fourteen teeth, and caved in his eye socket. You must have been beating him for a while before Detective Abbott got to you."

"I only hit him twice but my darkness was in control." Jake stared at the cast on his hand in wonder. "I would've killed him if the detective hadn't stopped me." He looked down and noticed his bandaged side. "So I did get shot. Do you know how bad I was hit?"

"I'm not supposed to but I do. You're going to recover but you lost a kidney."

"Damn."

"If I were a match, I'd give you one of mine."

Jake chuckled. "Thanks Jiao. It's a good thing I started with two." He reached out with his good hand. Jiao clasped it. "Are you okay?"

"I had a blood reaction to the spread of shrapnel – those little blades. They spent three hours removing the bits and I was awake the whole time." She smiled. "All I thought of during that surgery was putting my head on your chest as you carried me away from danger."

"I'll carry you anywhere Jiao."

"That would be nice."

Jake stared at Jiao. "There was no way Laksh was getting away after shooting you with that drone." He inhaled and winced. "Ouch. I am sore. I need to heal before I lift you again but, through all the fear, I loved carrying you through the park."

"I remember nothing but your strong arms around me after getting hit. That was the one time in my life I was helpless." Jiao wiped a tear from the corner of her eye. "You carried me. I will never forget it Jake."

"After I recover, I'd like to carry again – without all the danger."

"Where would you carry me to?"

"I'll carry you through the park again – just us. I'll lift you up, give you a passionate kiss, and carry you over the threshold and to a real bed. I'll carry you down the aisle if you're willing." He blushed, turned, and winced again. "I'll start by recovering and carrying you out of this hospital."

"I need to recover too. This blood reaction is slowing me down."

"Blood reaction? Is that why you have the drip?"

"Antibiotics." She looked at the drip. "I don't think they did as good a job on me as I did on you in removing shrapnel. They even said how they admired my work."

Jake nodded and smiled. "You are great. You've been amazing."

"So are you Jake and I can't wait for you to carry me over the threshold."

"Now that's motivation." He smiled. "Is it over? I mean with Laksh and the Azmis?"

"It's over. Laksh killed a homeless man before he got to you. That murder accelerated the investigation. When they searched the Golden Gate Park, they found the drones, the Chromebook, and my USB drive. They got all the information – on the patent, the Azmis, the ACES Corporation, the heroin, Laksh – everything."

"Are we cleared?"

Jiao nodded. "Yes. There was a man in a black van with Laksh. He tried to help Laksh but fled when he saw Detective Abbott." She chuckled. "So much for smart crooks. He drove straight to the ACES Corporation in Santa Clara. That's where they picked him up."

"We went to the right places."

"Yes we did. Because of the black van and our pictures, Detective Abbott and Detective Reed got warrants for both the ACES Corporation campus and the Azmis compound that day. They moved fast after the shooting in the park. Arjun and Lalita were so confident Laksh would succeed and have so many deep contacts, they never expected to be searched that afternoon. They never saw it coming. The police found more armed drones and more exploding buttons."

"Right there on the Azmi compound?"

"Yes and in that old fab next to the ACES Corporation, they found the thin film equipment used in manufacturing exotic weapons – including the RF-triggered exploding button."

"Wow," Jake whispered. "We really did it."

Jiao lifted Jake's hand and held it to her bosom. "I was so worried when you went after Laksh."

Jake nodded. "I had a dark force that I used against him. You didn't know about my dark side."

"I still don't. Do you want to tell me about it?"

"Not now. I need to keep that intoxicating darkness away. It can overtake someone with hate if they're not careful." He looked at Jiao. "My demon had me but it was thoughts of you that brought me back. It's hard to explain."

"Tell me when you're ready. We have time." She squeezed his hand. "I'll never forget what you did Jake."

He gripped Jiao's hand as if it were a lifeline. "And what about us?"

"If you want," Jiao whispered, "you've got me too."

Epilogue

State Senator Gita Bhatt stood at the podium in California's Sacramento capitol building. "The governor's traveling," Senator Bhatt said, "but he asked me to represent him and I am pleased to do so."

Jake stood next to Jiao absorbing the opulence of the California state capitol. The ceremony was on the capitol's second floor and, as Jake stared at the cast iron plaster and painted canvas ornamentation, the neoclassical fluted Corinthian columns, the varieties of Minerva statues, grizzly bears, and moldings that featured the never-to-be-emptied cornucopias; he wondered how anyone could do state business in such an ornate environment.

"We are pleased to present the highest citizen award our great state can bestow – the citizen's medal of valor. Doctor Jiao Liu and Mister Jake Hawes have distinguished themselves, in the face of great personal risk, by their fearless pursuit of justice. Because of their actions, the Azmis are in jail, California has distributed renewable energy contracts, and a new technology is sweeping the nation."

There was applause from the crowd. Jake looked at Jiao and nodded. His gaze fell to Hank who was standing behind them. The two exchanged a nod. He turned his gaze to the podium.

"I am proud to say, as a result of Doctor Liu and Mister Hawes's efforts as well as those of the late Amrish Cheena, there are two new energy storage companies in our great state. Both of these startups were conceived using the storage patent that our two awardees uncovered. These world changing products were conceived in Bay Area maker spaces by teenagers and crowd-funded into viable companies. We'll hear more about that but first, Doctor Jiao Liu and Mister Jake Hawes, please come up and accept your awards."

Jake motioned for Jiao to go first. They strode to the podium and stood side by side. Senator Bhatt first hung the medal on Jiao. She handed her a navy blue leather certificate case and shook her hand. "Congratulations Doctor Liu."

"Thank you."

Jake bent forward and the Senator draped the medal around his neck. He felt absurdly like Luke Skywalker getting the Medal of Bravery at the end of *Star Wars*. He stood and smiled. This was better than *Star Wars*, much better. His Han Solo was the beautiful Jiao Liu and she was smiling at him as he took his certificate case and shook the senator's hand.

The two awardees turned toward the crowd and basked in thunderous applause. Jake reached down and found Jiao's hand. He clasped it and raised their arms in a sign of their joint victory. The applause rose to a wave of adulation.

Jake and Jiao returned to their places. All those around them shook their hands in congratulations. Jake felt the heat of validation and love pulse through him. His smile broadened.

"Now, in honor of Amrish Cheena, we ask his sister Indira to come to the podium. We're launching state sponsored renewable energy company incubators in Amrish's honor. Although this amazing technology has led to startups in two other states, California aims to lead the country and the world in energy storage. These Amrish Cheena incubators will enable us to do just that. Indira, please come up."

Jake watched the sister of his old boss walk up to the podium. Indira shook hands with the senator and turned to the crowd. She presented the crowd a rueful smile. "I first want to thank and congratulate Jiao Liu and Jake Hawes for their outstanding and courageous work. Without them, my brother's death would've been for nothing. Without them California and the world would be in much worse shape."

She looked at the crowd and her eyes shone. "My brother Amrish wasn't perfect. We often talked about karma and what a strange and fickle thing it is . . ."

Jake felt Jiao squeeze his hand. He stared at Indira and thought he never heard truer words.

About the Author

Luke Marusiak is the author of the *Good Fight Series* historical fiction that follows five passionate characters who strive to make a difference from the turbulent 1960s to the turbulent 2010s. He also brought his passion for business to the *Excellence in Business Leadership Series*.

In this book, *The Patent*, Luke displayed his enthusiasm for technology in telling the tale of the struggle to control a patent with world changing potential.

Luke was raised in Western Pennsylvania. He served in the U.S. Army culminating with the 1st Infantry Division in Desert Storm. He worked in the Silicon Valley from the early 1990s working in semiconductors, hard drive media, and vacuum chamber systems in positions from process engineer to Chief Operating Officer and CEO. He draws on his family, friendships, and experiences for his writing. He currently resides in Washington with his wife.

For more information visit: www.lukemarusiak.com

68397384R00170

Made in the USA
Middletown, DE
03 April 2018